Gradually I began to realize the significance of all this. I didn't have to lift a finger. . . .

Nobody would ever tell me to iron my own shirt if I wanted it ironed.

Nobody would ever tell me, if we were out of, say, shampoo, "Go buy some. The walk will do you good."

*Nobody would ever tell me to clean my room.*

Servants would clean my room.

Laundresses would keep me supplied with ironed shirts.

Shampoo, bubbling bathwater, toasty fires, goat cheese delicacies — all would magically appear whenever I wanted them. A regiment of servants camped in the palace, primed to cater to my every whim, trained to provide me with every comfort, every luxury, everything my royal heart desired.

That's what being a princess means, I thought.

*What a deal.*

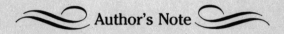 Author's Note

*This is a work of fiction. None of the characters are real. Saxony Coburn does not exist, and some of the "facts" about geography and aeronautics are obviously impossible.*

Ellen Conford

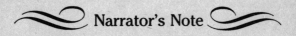

## Narrator's Note

*Disregard previous note. This is a true story. I know. I was there.*

Abby Adams
(Princess Florinda XIV of Saxony Coburn)

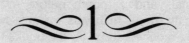

Right off the bat I have to say that no matter what you may have read in the papers, I don't think I was such a terrible princess. The media really sensationalized the whole thing.

I was not exiled from the principality of Saxony Coburn and I don't think it's fair to blame me for what ABC News called an "international incident." I mean, nobody in Washington even knew where Saxony Coburn was until I became princess of the place, so. . . .

But maybe that's not the best way to start.

Maybe I should start sixteen years ago, the day I was born. My parents were attending the Gloxinia Festival —

No. Nobody wants to read a long story about my parents' trip to Europe and my premature arrival in a tiny country where the only doctor was —

I guess the best thing to do is to start the story on the day I found out I was a princess.

It was a warm, sunny Friday in May, the weekend before finals and a month before my sixteenth birthday. My friend Josh was making sympathetic noises as I moaned about all the books I had piled in the backseat of his car.

"I cleaned out my whole locker," I said. "You should see it. It looks absolutely naked. And this is ridiculous. I know I'm not going to use all of them over the weekend, and I'll just have to lug them all back again, and lug them home and — oh, Josh, why can't I ever organize myself?"

"You'll be fine," he said calmly. "You're passing everything. Just do a little bit every day —"

"What every day? There's only Saturday and Sunday. Even if I start the minute I get home — I do this every time! I swear I won't, but I do. If only I'd started last week, like you did."

"You might have forgotten everything by now, like I did." He grinned. All of his books were piled in the backseat, too. His locker was as naked as mine.

I sighed. "This is going to be a very dismal weekend."

Josh pulled up to the curb in front of my house. Usually he swings right into the driveway, but today there was a big black car parked in front of the garage.

"Who's that?" he asked.

"I don't know. I hope nobody died. You want to come in for a while?"

"Are you kidding?" He turned around. "You see what we've got back there?" The seat was sagging under the combined weight of two hundred pounds of textbooks. "I shouldn't even have stopped. I should have just slowed down and let you jump out."

I hauled my books off the seat, piling them into my arms till I staggered under the load.

"You want some help getting into the house?" he offered.

"No thanks." I grunted. "I have to learn to do these things for myself." I straightened up and the books nearly hit my chin. "Don't worry," I said. "I can open the front door with my teeth."

He drove away with a wave and I trudged to the door. I glanced at the hearselike car in the driveway and began to worry that somebody really *had* died.

I managed to open the door with one hand, and nearly fell into the house. I kicked the door closed behind me and the load of books suddenly exploded from my aching arms like a volcano. As they crashed to the floor and scattered all over the hall, I heard my father say, "There she is now."

What's he doing home at this hour? I wondered. My mother came from the living room into the hall, stepping around the books and papers strewn on the floor. What's *she* doing home at this hour?

Why do her eyes look so red? Why is she putting her arm around my shoulders? Why isn't she saying,

"Don't leave your books lying around like that, Abby"?

I panicked. Somebody *was* dead. My parents were both here, but where was my brother, Teddy?

"Abby dear, come in here, will you?" She led me toward the living room.

"What's wrong?" I was shaking. "Where's Teddy? Who's dead?"

"Nobody's dead," my father said. "There's nothing wrong. You just have to prepare yourself for a little shock."

"Oh, God, tell me!" I cried. "What is it?"

I sank down onto the couch, and only then did I notice that there were two strange men standing on either side of the fireplace, staring at me. They looked very formal: black cutaway jackets and gray pants. On the mantle above the fireplace were two high silk hats.

The FBI! I thought wildly. Teddy's been kidnapped. They're in disguise. They plan to infiltrate the vicious gang of roving butlers who snatched my brother.

"If somebody doesn't tell me what's going on *this minute*," I screamed, "I'm going to scream!"

The two men bowed. "Your Highness," they said.

"Your what?" Did they say "Your Highness," or had I heard wrong? Did they say it to *me*?

"Listen, the prom is over already and I wasn't even a contender for prom queen, and anyway —"

My mother sat down beside me and took my hand. My father sat down on the other side of me and took my other hand.

"This is Monsieur Creanga," my father said. The man on the right bowed again. "And this is Monsieur Blitzen." The man on the left bowed again. They looked like bobbing dashboard dolls. I wondered where Donder was.

"They're emissaries from the principality of Saxony Coburn. You remember we told you about Saxony Coburn?"

Emissaries — that didn't sound terrible. I began to calm down a little. At least it explained the big black car. It didn't explain anything else.

"Yes, I remember about Saxony Coburn. That's where I was born. During the Gloxinia Festival."

Whenever my parents tell the story of my month-early birth, I crack up. So does everyone else who hears the story. It was so crazy, and Saxony Coburn sounded so quaint and corny, that the whole incident could have been the plot of an ancient Hollywood musical.

It seems that my parents decided to have a last fling before I was born, and went on a three-week tour of Europe two months before my mother was scheduled to deliver.

They never planned to visit Saxony Coburn — they'd never heard of Saxony Coburn — but the travel agent threw it in for free, so they figured, Why not? They would arrive just in time for the Gloxinia Festival. (The gloxinia was Saxony Coburn's national flower.) They were told that the whole place was so picturesque and old-world that they would love it.

The only way to get into the country was by goat

cart, which they were *not* told. The country had no airport and no rail service, and the region approaching the capital city of Dulsia (the only town in Saxony Coburn) was mountainous and completely unpaved.

The way my father tells it, either I did not enjoy the trip up through the rocky, one-lane road, or my mother's obstetrician was lousy at math. Within two hours of their arrival in Saxony Coburn, just as the floats were parading past the royal palace, my mother went into labor.

"What could I do?" my father always asks. "I led her right across the square, cut through the parade between the floats celebrating Saxony Coburn's past and Saxony Coburn's present — which looked exactly the same, by the way — and brought her into the palace."

"And we thought it was a miracle," my mother says, "because the first person we saw as we walked into the palace was a doctor, who had just delivered the princess's baby. He was about to announce the joyful news to the crowd, but when he saw my condition, he agreed that the joyful news could wait ten minutes."

The doctor was pretty joyful himself, according to my father. He'd been celebrating the royal birth with elderberry wine when my parents showed up.

So I was born in the servants' kitchen, and my parents stayed for five days while my mother recuperated and the doctor was sure it was safe for me to travel. Unfortunately this meant that they missed their goat cart connection to the bus that would take them to the train that would get them to France and their flight home — which they also missed. But my father said I saved them a bundle in hospital bills.

Who could forget a story like that? Now, as I sat between them on the couch, I nodded impatiently. "Yes, of course I remember."

"And you remember that you were born on the same day that the princess was born?" my mother asked.

I nodded, and looked up at Donder and Blitzen, who were gazing at me like I was a long-lost relative.

"Your Highness," M. Blitzen began.

"Stop calling me — oh, no! No, you're not going to tell me that I was switched at birth with the princess and I'm really — and she's really —" I broke up. I began giggling uncontrollably.

I turned to my father. "I know you like a good joke every once in a while, but this is really your finest hour."

I stood up and strolled over to the fireplace. "Mr. Blitzen," I said. "Mr. Donder —"

"Creanga, Your Highness."

"Whatever. Nice try, but it didn't work. Why don't you return the suits and the car to wherever you rented them, and maybe they won't charge you for the whole day."

"Abby," my father said, "this isn't a joke."

"You were terrific, too, Mom. That little bit of red around your eyelids — nice touch."

"Oh, Abby!" She burst into tears.

My father cleared his throat. I looked at the

expressions on their faces, at my mother's tears, and I didn't think I would make it back to the couch before I fainted.

"Your Highness, it seems there was a little mix-up," M. Creanga began.

"This is ridiculous!" I yelled. "These things don't really happen. Only in the movies. You are *not* going to tell me that I'm really the princess of Saxony Coburn."

"The doctor who delivered you and the princess — that is, you and Abby Adams, the American child —"

"I'm Abby Adams," I insisted.

"I beg your pardon, Your Highness, but Doctor Zdenka, who delivered the two babies, died last week, leaving a letter with his nurse which was to be opened after his death. The letter confesses the whole shameful episode."

"The doctor took full responsibility for the confusion," M. Blitzen went on. "He suffered terrible guilt to his dying day."

"Well, I should think so!" I snapped.

"And he never took another drop of elderberry wine. . . ."

I started to giggle again. "This is too much. I mean, *really*. The whole bit, with the elderberry wine and everything. Now you're going to tell me that I have to go back to Saxony Coburn and take my rightful place as heir to the throne."

For a terrible moment there was nothing but silence.

M. Blitzen and M. Creanga exchanged troubled

glances. My mother and father exchanged troubled glances.

My father cleared his throat. "That's exactly what they're going to tell you," he said.

"You mean, I really am a princess?" I asked. "I'm not your daughter?"

"You'll always be our daughter!" my mother declared, and burst into tears.

That's when I began to believe them.

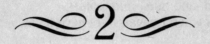

M. Donder and M. Creanga went on talking and my mother went on sniffling. I only heard about half of what they said, partly because I was in shock, and partly because I was already sorting out the implications of all this in my mind.

The two royal emissaries were trying to persuade me to leave my parents, give up my normal life, and take on a whole new identity as Princess Florinda XIV of Saxony Coburn.

Of course it was impossible. I'm not princess material. I don't look anything like the beautiful princesses in the fairy tales I used to love. I've got the blonde hair and the blue eyes, but I'm no raving beauty. I'm a reasonably pleasant-looking, average American teenager.

Besides, the whole idea was so scary.

How could I leave my family, leave Kansas, leave my country, my friends? How could I adapt to a completely different culture, a backwards little country that was accessible only by goat cart? They probably didn't even have cable TV.

They expected me to live in a palace and be princess of this place? I didn't even know what language they spoke. How would I go to school if I couldn't speak the language? And what about veterinary school?

Besides, I had all those finals next week.

" . . . adoptive parents are welcome to accompany you," M. Blitzen was saying. "We realize this is quite a shock, Your Highness, and of course, Her Most Serene Highness, your mother, wishes to make your transition as comfortable as possible under the circumstances."

That, at least, was reassuring. When Her Most Serene Highness, my mother, was unreasonable about something, I could always go to my mother, the commoner, and complain.

"You know perfectly well we can't uproot ourselves like that," my father said angrily. "I'm sure you've done plenty of research on us. Lynn and I have jobs. We're not royalty, and we need the money. We have a son —"

"Hi. What's going on?" My eleven-year-old brother Teddy walked into the room right on cue and stared at the two strange men in front of the fireplace. "You talking about me?"

"They're talking about me," I said. "I'm Princess Florinda XIV of Saxony Coburn."

"And I'm King Zaxor of Mars," Teddy said. "The king is hungry. The king needs a peanut butter fix." The king went into the kitchen.

My father stood up, his face tight with anger. "I think this has gone far enough. Abby is fifteen years old, she's a United States citizen, and if you take her against her will you'll be guilty of kidnapping — not to mention an act of aggression that could lead to war."

"Mr. Adams, please."

Gee. Think of that. A war between America and Saxony Coburn over *me*. Just like Helen of Troy. I didn't imagine Saxony Coburn had any nuclear weapons, so I figured it would be a pretty minor skirmish with hardly any casualties except maybe for a couple of goats.

"Mr. Adams, the princess is not a United States citizen, she is a citizen of Saxony Coburn. And in Saxony Coburn, she is not a minor."

My mother faced M. Creanga as if she were trying to stare him down. "We have her birth certificate," she said.

"And we have evidence that it's the wrong birth certificate," he replied. "Your State Department agrees."

"You've been to the State Department?" she demanded. "And they said you could take our daughter?"

"I'm calling our congressman," my father announced. "This is outrageous."

Suddenly I found myself intrigued with the whole

16

nutty situation. All these people fighting over me made me feel awfully important. Sure, my parents loved me, but here was an entire *country* — even if it was only twenty-two square miles — clamoring for me to return to my homeland and lead them.

Everybody was standing around the fireplace, bickering, and I was sitting alone, on the couch, sort of as if I were on a throne, and I got the first tantalizing sense of what it would be like to be a Most Serene Highness.

I smiled, most serenely, at my parents and my subjects.

"Maybe," I said, "we can work something out."

My parents stared as if they didn't know what had gotten into me. That made three of us. All I knew was that these guys were making me an offer I might not be able to refuse — at least, not without thinking it over.

To be a princess, with my own palace, to be famous and loved by my subjects, to get everything I wanted with just a wave of my royal hand — I could really *live* all the fairy-tale dreams of my childhood.

I didn't know if I'd stay there happily ever after, but I could try it out for a year, and then if I didn't like being a princess, I'd abdicate.

I stood up regally. "Shall we go into the kitchen?"

Teddy was eating a peanut butter sandwich and watching a rerun of *Leave it to Beaver* on the little TV. "Hey, Princess, your crown is tilted."

I ignored him and turned to my parents. They looked absolutely stricken.

"Listen," I began, "I know it's all crazy, and I

know you can't come with me and I'll miss you, but a part of me really wants to do this."

"Half an hour ago you said —"

"Daddy, I was in shock. I really haven't had a chance to think about it, but I'm starting to. I'm asking myself, How can I pass up an experience like this? I mean, could *you*?"

"Easily," he retorted. "If I had to leave my family forever —"

"Who said anything about forever? Look, we have exchange students from Japan and Nigeria in school. If I had the chance to be an exchange student in Nigeria or someplace, you wouldn't stop me. You'd probably say it was the chance of a lifetime."

"But Abby," my mother said, "this *is* for a lifetime. It's not like being an exchange student at all."

"Mom, if I don't like it I can always abdicate. They can't stop me from giving up the throne. I mean, I'll be the *princess*. They can't stop me from anything, except maybe filching the crown jewels when I exile myself back to America."

Teddy had turned the sound way down on the TV. He didn't stop eating, but he was chewing very slowly.

"I know I'll miss you both something awful." I tilted my head in Teddy's direction. "I might even miss him. But I can call you every week, and you can come to visit on vacations, or maybe they'll let me come visit you here, and if I can't hack it, I'll just step down. Let's at least think about it some more before we give them a definite answer."

My parents exchanged another one of those looks. I wondered if they were disappointed in me. Maybe they thought I didn't love them enough to stay in Kansas and just be their daughter, average American Abby, veterinarian-to-be. I hoped my mother wouldn't clutch me to her bosom and sob, "Where have we failed?"

But that's not my mother's style.

"You're asking us to give you up," she said quietly.

"But you'd have to give me up when I went to college."

"It's not the same thing," my father said. "What if you decide you like being royalty? What if you decide to stay there for the rest of your life?"

Teddy put down his sandwich. "*She's* royalty?"

"I told you. I'm Princess Florinda XIV of Saxony Coburn. Those men in the living room want to take me back to my throne."

"This isn't a joke? And you're all in on it except me?"

My father shook his head.

Teddy gaped. "You're *going*?"

"I haven't really decided for sure yet."

He stared at the three of us. "Well," he said finally, "you'll make a great princess."

"Thank you," I said.

"You're sure bossy enough."

Somehow I really had made up my mind by then to go to Saxony Coburn, but we talked for almost two hours after the emissaries left. I think my parents wanted mostly to be sure that I knew what I was doing, and to try and accept the reality of the situation, which wasn't easy for any of us.

It had to be even harder for them than for me, I

realized, because I was getting more and more excited about the idea, and the more excited I got, the more depressed they looked.

I knew that if I wanted to go and be a princess, they couldn't stop me. The U.S. government sided with Saxony Coburn, so they wouldn't do anything to prevent it. I was of age according to the laws of Saxony Coburn, so, short of locking me in my room, there was no way to keep me here in Kansas.

But I didn't say any of these things. Even if they weren't my "real" parents — and that was the hardest thing of all for me to believe — I didn't want to pull royal rank on them.

However, I got a severe jolt when they told me I'd have to leave on Sunday.

*"This* Sunday? You mean, the day after tomorrow?"

I wouldn't have time to pack, to say good-bye to my friends, to make a farewell tour of Middleton, to hold onto my mother and father before I had to let them go.

I got this sudden flash of how much I would miss everything I was leaving. A dull, hollow ache formed in the pit of my stomach. I was already homesick and I hadn't even left home yet.

What would I do without Josh and Carol, my closest friends? What would I do without my mother and father? Who would I talk to? Who would I hug? Who would hug *me*? Would I be allowed to go to school and mingle with commoners, or would I have to sit on a throne all day? The thought of a year without friends, without dates, without my family, was sobering enough to make me forget for a moment all the exciting things that being a princess meant.

I eyed Teddy, who was sitting on the piano bench. "Hey," I said, "you want to come with me?"

I was only half joking.

"Carol?" I clutched the telephone receiver to my ear so hard that my fingers hurt.

"Oh, hi, Ab. How many finals are you going to flunk? I have it figured, two for sure, and three if they ask me anything about the Civil War that wasn't in *Gone with the Wind*."

"Finals! I forgot all about them."

"You forgot about finals? You're putting me on."

"Carol, don't say 'You're putting me on' until you hear why I forgot about them."

I told her why.

There was dead silence at Carol's end of the phone when I finished the story.

Then, "Abby?"

"Yeah?"

"Now can I say it?"

I sighed. "Go ahead."

*"You're putting me on."*

"Josh? You have to come over."

"Now? You know I can't. I'm up to my neck in inert gases. In fact, I may be over my head. Choke, choke."

"Josh," I said, "this is more important than inert gases. This is more important than finals."

"Hey, that car *wasn't* a hearse, was it?" he asked.

"No. Nobody died. We're all alive."

"Thank God. In that case, I'll see you Monday."

"No," I said sadly, "you won't see me Monday. That's just it."

"What are you talking about?"

"Josh," I began, "you're not going to believe this. . . ."

# 3

"Can't we at least stop and look around a little?" I asked irritably. "I didn't even get to see Paris, except for the airport."

"I'm sorry, Mademoiselle, but we have to make the helicopter connection."

*"Helicopter?"*

"I know you must be tired, Your Highness, but we are on the last leg of the journey. And you did get to ride on the famed Orient Express. It's just a few miles by automobile to the heliport, and then, before you know it, you'll be home."

"Heliport? I thought we'd go by bus, and then a nice goat cart —"

"Oh, no, Mademoiselle. These are modern times,

and you are our princess. I'm sure you'll find the helicopter trip much less arduous than a goat cart."

"Look," I said, my voice shaking, "I don't know how to tell you this, but I can't be Princess Florinda after all. Nobody told me I'd have to ride in a helicopter. I've hardly ever been on a plane, except for the flight to Paris. I mean, okay, once, to Disney World, and we visited my aunt and uncle in New York, but that's only a few hours, and the planes had doors. I've seen pictures of helicopters. They don't have any doors! *You can fall out of helicopters!*"

"Oh, not this one, Your Highness. We rented a very big one. I'm sure it has doors."

"You *rented* a helicopter?" For a moment, at least, I forgot I was terrified. "The royal family of Saxony Coburn *rents* its helicopters?"

"We only use them occasionally," M. Blitzen said, "and as Chancellor of the Exchequer, I advised that it was more economical to rent the machine when we needed it than to maintain one all year round."

"Well, I'm going to save you the cost of renting this one, because there is no way you're going to get me up in it."

I folded my arms across my chest and faced them down as regally as I could. They held a hurried, whispered consultation in French, and I began to tap my foot. I thought it added a nice touch of haughty impatience.

"We have devised a Plan B, Mademoiselle," M. Creange said. M. Blitzen scurried off. "While he is ⬚⬚⬚ e arrangements, wouldn't you like coffee ⬚⬚⬚ nice pastry? There's a shop right over

"What arrangements is he making?"

"He will attempt to rent a limousine and have us met at the border by a jeep. It will take longer this way, and it is not quite the dignified arrival we had planned, but. . . ." He heaved a dramatic sigh.

"There'd be nothing dignified," I said, as we sat down in the coffee shop, "in having me fall out of the helicopter and throw up on the welcoming throng."

M. Creanga ordered coffee and some sort of pastry and I looked around the tiny shop. Coffee shops and airport waiting rooms were about all the sights I had seen in the last fourteen hours.

Sure, I'd ridden on the famed Orient Express, but that was in the middle of the night, and I didn't even get to see any scenery. The train had a nifty dining car, right out of the 1920's, but it didn't make up for the tedium of the rest of the trip. A nice Agatha Christie-type murder would have helped, but no such luck.

The waitress brought us our coffee and little squares of gooey, honey-covered pastry. I shoved my stereo box under the table between my feet. There had been so little time to pack, I took only the barest essentials. My parents would ship everything else later.

I had my stereo, two suitcases filled with the most vital cosmetics and makeup, and whatever clothes we could stuff in them.

"This is delicious," I said, my mouth full of pastry. "What is it?"

"Baklava. I'm glad you like it, Your Highness."

"Mmm." I took a sip of coffee. I nearly choked. I

hardly ever drink coffee, but I was so tired I thought the caffeine might help.

"This is terrible!" It was thick, black, and bitter, with the consistency of mud.

"Turkish coffee, Mademoiselle. Quite strong. Add some sugar."

"There isn't enough sugar in the world to make this drinkable. Never mind." I pushed the cup away.

M. Creanga took a little silver flask out of his pocket. "Perhaps a touch of elderberry wine?"

"Are you kidding? Elderberry wine is what got me into this mess in the first place!"

Just then M. Blitzen bustled in. Apparently he had succeeded in renting something at the Belgrade Avis, or wherever we were. I poured about half a cup of sugar into the coffee and took a sip. It still tasted awful, but I was so tired I was ready to tilt over onto my baklava.

"If you will finish your coffee and pastry, Mademoiselle, the limousine is ready."

I snapped my eyes open and blinked a few times. I popped the rest of the baklava into my mouth. I gulped down the remains of the little cup of coffee.

It didn't taste so bad this time. Maybe it was the honey from the pastry, or all that sugar I had added, or maybe you just had to get used to it. I even drank the dark, sugary dregs at the bottom of the cup.

M. Blitzen took my arm and helped me out of the chair, which was a good thing, because suddenly I was so weak I didn't think I could walk. My knees felt wobbly and my head seemed too heavy for my neck to support it.

"My stereo," I mumbled. "Don't forget my stereo."

M. Creanga reached under the table for the box. His silver flask was still on the table. He capped it and put it in his pocket.

Isn't that strange? I thought, as M. Blitzen steered me around the tables. When did he open the flask? I didn't remember him drinking from it, or pouring anything into his coffee —

"You drugged me!" I shrieked. I twisted out of M. Blitzen's grasp. "You put something in my coffee!" I staggered a little and M. Blitzen put his arm around my waist to steady me, just before I fell over a man reading a newspaper.

"Mademoiselle, please!" M. Creanga looked around nervously. "You are merely exhausted from the trip. I put nothing in your coffee. I could not do such a thing."

"You did! You did, you put something in my coffee, and I'll bet you're going to bundle me up and toss me in a helicopter like a sack of goat chow."

I started to cry.

How could my mother let me go off halfway around the world with two men she had never seen before? Here she'd spent most of my formative years warning me never to take candy from strangers, and now she'd blithely sent me away with a pair of the strangest strangers I'd ever seen.

"Take your hands off my royal person!" I slapped at M. Blitzen.

"Your Highness, I am afraid that if I let go of you, you will fall to the floor and injure yourself."

"If you don't let go of me you're going to need the world's biggest Band-Aid!"

He let go of me. I grabbed the back of a chair. I didn't feel so sleepy now; fear can do that. But my knees still wobbled. My voice carried, but I didn't know if my legs would.

"Mademoiselle," M. Creanga pleaded, "I swear on the life of Her Most Serene Highness that I put nothing in your coffee. You are simply fatigued. You will sleep in the limousine and feel much refreshed."

He sounded sincere. For a Saxony Coburnian, swearing on my mother, the princess, was probably a pretty serious oath. His deep, gray eyes looked reproachful, as if I had insulted him.

I peered nervously around the shop. The few customers were calmly sipping their coffee and munching their sandwiches. Even the man I had almost fallen over paid absolutely no attention to me.

"I'm yelling," I whimpered, "and nobody's doing anything. They're ignoring us. You could be kidnapping me and they're not lifting a finger."

"This is the Balkans, Your Highness," M. Creanga said gently. "The people tend to be rather blasé about minor political scuffles."

My shoulders slumped. "All right. Okay. Take me to the limousine. I guess I have to trust you. It's not going to do any good to yell for help."

"May I assist you?" M. Blitzen offered.

I didn't feel so fuzzy-headed as he led me out of the coffee shop and back into the bustling train station.

"I guess you were telling the truth about not drugging me," I said to M. Creanga. "I mean, I'm weak, but it must just be jet lag. Or goat-cart lag. Yeah, goat-cart lag. That's it. I'm making jokes," I babbled. "See, my head is clear now, otherwise I couldn't make these terrific jokes, right?"

"Of course, Your Highness."

"Jeep lag! Yeah, jeep lag. You told me the truth about everything," I decided, "so I guess you really did get a jeep. Nothing to worry about." How nice they were. Why had I thought they were the least bit dangerous?

I was their princess. They catered to my every wish. They were doing everything to make this trip as easy as possible for me. They even switched plans at the last minute, so I could ride in a jeep instead of the rented helicopter.

M. Creanga cleared his throat. "There is one thing, Your Highness." He shifted his eyes away from mine, as if he couldn't face me.

I stopped in front of a poster of a smiling peasant girl in native costume, draping red flowers over a lamb.

"What?" Suddenly I felt panic building up again. *"What?"*

M. Creanga lowered his head and seemed unable to take his eyes off his gleaming patent leather shoes.

"I fibbed about the jeep."

*"Help!"*

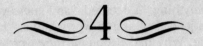

I didn't see much of Yugoslavia as we left the city and sped down the open highway toward the heliport. Facing almost certain death, I was preoccupied with watching my entire life pass before my eyes.

What I recalled mostly was the last hectic thirty-six hours I'd spent as a commoner. Things had happened so fast, that even in my mind's eye the images seemed like a movie run at double-speed.

Josh came over Friday night and we went out for Big Macs. We sat in the front seat of the dark car, eating, and Teddy sat in the back, poking his straw into his thick shake.

"My last Big Mac," I said mournfully. "Can you

believe I'm going to a place that doesn't have a McDonald's?"

"After this weekend I can believe anything," Josh said. He watched me devour the Big Mac. "I can hardly eat a bite of this. I hope you're going to miss me more than you'll miss burgers."

"Of course I will." I lowered my voice. "I'll even miss the id-kay."

"The id-kay will miss you, too," said Teddy.

Josh sighed. "You know, I think I took our friendship too much for granted. Maybe we take everything too much for granted."

"I know what you mean. You think things will last forever. The people you love will always be there, things will go on the way they always have — and then all of a sudden they don't."

Josh stuffed his uneaten burger into a bag. "Let's get out of here before I start blubbering."

"I'm going to cry whether we get out of here or not," I sniffled.

"I'm not going to cry," Teddy declared. He made loud slurping noises with his straw.

"Oh yes you will, my man," Josh said. "Yes you will."


I fell asleep on the way to the heliport. I awoke to find that the limousine had stopped in the middle of a large, open field. White-capped mountains rose in the distance. Twenty feet from the car a small flock of sheep milled around, nibbling at the grass at the edge of the tarmac.

The sheep didn't seem the least bit disturbed by the roaring noise that came from somewhere behind us. I was a little confused, because a minute ago I had been dreaming that it was Saturday night, and my parents were trying to call the State Department, and now I was gazing dopily at a bunch of sheep bumping into each other.

My first thought was of the poster in the railroad station. I wondered why the cheerful peasant girl wasn't here twining flowers around her flock.

"We have arrived, Your Highness," announced M. Blitzen. The driver opened the door of the car to help me out.

"This is it? My whole kingdom?" I could barely hear my own words over the roar of the wind.

I turned around to survey my domain, and screamed.

The roar that drowned my words was not from the stiff wind that whipped my hair and made my coat flap against my legs.

In front of a row of broad, gray sheds, a huge helicopter gleamed silver in the sun, its snub nose pointed at me, its rotor blades whirling lethally.

"We are not in Saxony Coburn yet," M. Blitzen shouted. "This is where we pick up the helicopter."

I toyed with the idea of refusing to budge; I could scrounge up a native costume and stay at the edge of the tarmac forever, tending the sheep and posing for an occasional travel poster.

But the driver was already hauling my stuff out of the limousine, and Donder and Blitzen each had me by an elbow, and, practically speaking, sheep-herding had never been high on my list of career choices.

The helicopter door slid open — at least it had

a door — and a rope ladder dropped down.

"I can't climb a rope!" I yelled. "I almost flunked gym two semesters in a row because I couldn't do rope-climbing!"

"It is a very sturdy ladder," M. Blitzen assured me.

I sighed. I started up the ladder after him. I felt my feet slip on a couple of the rungs. I was definitely not wearing rope-ladder-climbing shoes.

I fell into the helicopter. M. Blitzen helped me into a seat behind the pilot. M. Creanga climbed in after us and sat down.

"You see, Your Highness," he said, "it's a very big helicopter."

"It'll never get off the ground," I muttered.

The pilot hauled the rope ladder up, and slid the door shut. He grinned broadly at me and said something like, "Strits clika."

"Fasten your seat belt," M. Creanga translated.

I fastened my seat belt. I squeezed my eyes shut. I clenched my fists in my lap. The pilot chuckled and hummed to himself.

"Why is he so *cheerful*?" I demanded. "I want to smell his breath before we take off."

Suddenly I felt this little swaying motion, and there was nothing under the helicopter but air. My eyes flew open. We were hovering above the sheep, who finally had the good sense to go stumbling over each other away from the tarmac.

I screamed.

The pilot turned to look at me. He began talking rapidly, gesturing with one hand and flashing encouraging little grins.

"Tell him to turn around and watch the road!"

I clamped my eyes shut again.

We seemed to be going straight up. My stomach was still down on the tarmac. I whimpered with terror. My heart was pounding so hard and fast that I was afraid I really would die. Of fright.

Oh, God, I prayed silently, why didn't you let me stay with the sheep?

"Are we there yet?"

"We have only just ascended, Your Highness."

"You *said* it would be a short trip!"

I felt a tiny bit less hysterical when we stopped rising straight up — which I don't think is aerodynamically possible — and started flying toward the mountains.

At least, that's where M. Creanga said we were headed. I kept my eyes closed.

"You are missing a very thrilling ride," M. Blitzen said. "I think if you would open your eyes you would find the natural beauty of the scenery below quite enchanting."

"I don't want to see scenery below me," I said tightly. "I want to see scenery *above* me. And when I take over the throne, I'm going to have you both beheaded."

Someone sighed. "There is no death penalty in Saxony Coburn," M. Creanga said. "But I believe I comprehend the full extent of Her Highness's displeasure."

Saturday morning, the day before I left Kansas, Carol and I had tried to find some information about Saxony Coburn. That is, in between crying

34

jags and solemn oaths to write to each other every week.

The *Britannica* had two brief paragraphs, but they mostly covered history and geography. We found that Saxony Coburn became a principality in 1716, was located in central Europe, and had been a neutral country, like Switzerland, since 1812.

The only other mention of the place we could find was in a reference book in the children's section of the library. There was a whole page on Saxony Coburn that gave me a sketchy idea of the flavor of the country. The book had a little map and a photograph of the royal palace taken during a Gloxinia Festival parade.

"It looks so picturesque," Carol said. "Spanish tile roof, Moorish arches, flying buttresses, gargoyles. Now that's a palace with *style*."

"A lot of styles," I agreed. "But the country sounds so small. Twenty-two square miles. What is that in acres?"

A little box at the top of the page contained "Facts and Figures About Saxony Coburn." I read every word. The head of the government was the princess.

"That's me," I pointed out proudly. "I mean, it will be me, eventually."

The official language was French.

"Uh oh," said Carol.

The principal export products were gloxinias, elderberry wine, stamps, sausage skins, and plastic raincoats.

"Plastic raincoats?" I wondered. *"Plastic raincoats?"*

I had approximately sixteen thousand loyal subjects.

"It doesn't say anything about TV," I noted gloomily.

"They probably didn't think that was important enough to mention," Carol replied.

Remembering this now, in the helicopter, I was about to ask M. Creanga whether my country had TV or not, when he said, "We are approaching Saxony Coburn, Your Highness. We will be there in a few minutes."

"If you open your eyes," M. Blitzen said, "you will get your first look at your native land. The view from the air is quite breathtaking. It will be a sight you will treasure for the rest of your life."

I thought the rest of my life might be extremely short — like five minutes — but I opened my eyes. Once I opened them, I couldn't help staring through the windows in fascination.

We were flying between two mountains. Patches of snow and ice dotted the slopes, which were thick with evergreens and brush. I figured we couldn't be too high up, but when I looked down, I saw we were high enough.

"Eek," I commented. I took a few deep breaths to steady myself. Only moments from now I would be greeting my subjects. It wouldn't do to have them think that their princess, who would lead them out of the nineteenth century into high-tech industrialization and cable TV, was a coward.

The copter started to descend.

"Eek!" I clutched at my stomach as if I were in a

plunging elevator. We weren't dropping that fast, actually, but it was a weird feeling.

"There, Your Highness. You can see Saxony Coburn now."

Below us was a sort of plateau. As the ground came up to meet us and everything grew larger and larger, I could see a red roof, which I thought must be the palace, and a very large, grayish area in front of it. That had to be the palace square.

"I think I see the palace," I said excitedly, "but where else should I look? There's no red outline like there is on the map."

"The royal palace is at the east end of the capital city of Dulsia. To the north, you can make out our industrial area. That large white building with the tin roof is our raincoat factory."

"I meant to ask you about that," I began, but we were dropping lower and lower. Now I could make out the tiles on the palace roof. The square in front looked like cobblestones. I wondered how the helicopter was going to land with all those people milling around.

"Ohh, this is so exciting!" I squealed. "I can't believe it!"

I twisted back and forth in the seat and saw horses and little white cottages, and farms and goats and a glittering blue lake.

"Did all those people come to see me?"

"The schools and shops are closed, Your Highness. Today is a national holiday."

Wow! A national holiday, just for me. Wait till Teddy hears about this. We were low enough now that I could pick out my mother, the princess, standing in front of the massive oak doors of the palace.

I recognized her right away. She was the one with the crown.

"I'm so *nervous*."

The helicopter hovered as a cordon of men in red and black uniforms herded the crowd back from the square.

"Just smile and wave, Your Highness," M. Creanga said. "They will love you. They have been waiting for you ever since the scandal was revealed."

Scandal? What scandal?

Maybe this was more serious than I had thought. What if there were palace intrigues? Or a military takeover? Those men in the red and black uniforms — were they happy in their work, or were they simply biding their time until the revolution?

And where, I wondered, was the other me? I mean, the real Abby Adams, the pretender to my throne? She wasn't with the royal family. A tall man with a black beard stood next to the princess, so I assumed he was the prince. But there was no teenager with them, only two little girls with bouquets of flowers.

The helicopter landed, bouncing a couple of times on the cobblestones. I was too overwhelmed now to be afraid. Besides, we were on the ground. How far could I fall?

"Are we going to do the rope ladder bit?" I asked, as the doors slid open. "Is that your idea of a dignified arrival?"

"No, no, Mademoiselle," M. Blitzen said. "We have a ramp."

Sure enough, two men in white jump suits were rolling a little iron staircase up to the door of the helicopter. Did they rent the staircase, too?

"We will go first, Your Highness," M. Creanga said. He had to shout to be heard over the cheers of the crowd, which were so loud they nearly drowned out the noise made by the whirling rotor blades. "Then you stand for a few seconds on the top step, and wave to the crowd. This will give the journalists a photo opportunity. Then walk down the steps and greet the princess and prince, who will be standing in front of the barriers. Do you know how to curtsey?"

"I can fake it," I said. "Let's get this over with before I chicken out."

M. Creanga took my stereo and pocketbook, so I would have my hands free for waving and other royal formalities. They climbed out of the helicopter and the roar of the crowd grew even louder.

I took a deep breath and ducked out the door to stand on the top steps of the ramp.

*"VIVE FLORINDA! VIVE LA PRINCESSE!"*

The mob shrieked and strained forward against the red velvet rope barricades. Hundreds of faces bobbed and jumped in front of me, hundreds of arms waved wildly. Children perched on their parents' shoulders clutching flags with a purple gloxinia emblazoned on a white background, the flag I had seen in the library book.

The princess and prince stood facing the helicopter, the prince stroking his beard, the princess — my *mother* — squinting a little in the sun.

My stomach fluttered wildly. I stood on the top step of the ramp, gripping the white railing as if I were paralyzed. I forced my lips into a smile and waved. The roar from the crowd was deafening.

Two uniformed men carried something to the bottom of the ramp and bent down. A red carpet spilled open. The guards positioned themselves on opposite sides of the carpet and snapped to attention. A little girl with a bouquet of flowers tiptoed to the edge of the carpet and waited.

Somewhere a brass band struck up a dignified march.

I didn't need a princess instruction manual to recognize my cue.

I was so nervous I was afraid I wouldn't be able to make it down the ramp. Flashbulbs popped, my new parents shaded their eyes from the sun, and I could see handmade signs in the crowd. *"BIEN-VENUE, FLORINDA!"* "WELCOME HOME, FLOR-INDA!" *"NOTRE PRINCESSE!"*

Many of the people were dressed in what must have been native costumes. Despite the glaring sun, almost everybody was wearing plastic raincoats. My subjects all seemed to be swathed in Saran Wrap.

I took one more deep breath and started down the steps.

"All in all," said Princess Florinda XIII, "a very successful homecoming." She patted my hand. "Don't you think so, Albert?"

"Yes, my sweet." The prince nodded. He patted my other hand. "The people were obviously overjoyed to greet our little Dolores."

Dolores? Who's Dolores? I thought I was Florinda XIV.

I'd clear up the name business later. Right now, at tea with my royal parents in the morning room, I was tired, scared, homesick, and cold.

It was a pretty fancy tea. I mean, when they said, "We'll have tea," they didn't just hand me a cup with hot water and a tea bag in it. The table was set out with sandwiches, cakes, goat-cheese tarts, cold roast meat, hot muffins, and elderberry wine. All the sandwiches had trimmed crusts. I think I ate fourteen sandwiches.

There was a fire in the fireplace, but it didn't seem to make the large, dim room any cozier. It was much colder inside the palace than it was outside in the sun.

I guess it was a successful homecoming, if you measured it by decibel level and enthusiasm. In fact, some of the depression I was beginning to feel was probably caused by the contrast between the thrilling unreality of my brass band reception and the chilly reality of sitting in a huge palace with two unknown people who were supposed to be "Mom" and "Dad."

I felt like a street cleaner after a ticker-tape parade. When all the excitement is over, what you're faced with is an empty street and a whole lot of cleaning up.

I was relieved to find out that the prince and princess spoke English.

"We can even speak the slang," the princess assured me.

"We watch American movies all the time," the prince said. "That Humphrey Bogart is one cool cat."

The first things I'd packed were my French book and a dictionary. I'd imagined walking around with the dictionary hanging by a rope from my waist, and having to refer to it every time someone spoke to me.

But now, sitting at tea, a common language didn't seem very important, since I couldn't think of a word to say to them. I had a million questions, but none of them seemed very urgent, either, when all I could feel was this incredible fatigue, and a longing for my own, modest, centrally heated house.

The questions that loomed largest in my mind were: What time is it now in America? What is my mother making for dinner? What is Teddy watching on TV? How are Josh and Carol doing on their finals?

I didn't even know what time it was here.

"What time is it?" I asked.

The prince took out a pocket watch and snapped it open.

"Nearly five-thirty," he said.

"Oh, Albert, how thoughtless we are!" the princess said. "Poor Dolores must be exhausted after her long journey. She needs a nice hot bath and a good night's sleep. We have been selfish, thinking only of our own joy in seeing you, my dear."

"No, really, that's okay." At least they have indoor plumbing, I thought. "I wanted to meet you, too."

They seemed very nice. My mother was older than my mother — I mean, my mother, the princess, was about ten years older than my mother, the commoner. Without her crown she looked like a very ordinary, middle-aged lady.

The prince had a dark, spade-shaped beard speckled with gray, and he was dressed in some sort of military uniform, with a gold band across his chest and a whole lot of medals and ribbons on his white coat.

I guess I expected them to be wearing ermine capes or something, but the princess wore a simple blue dress that matched her eyes, and a fuzzy blue shawl around her shoulders.

"Would you know what time it is in America?" I asked.

The prince raised his wrist, pushed something on his watch, and said, "Twelve-thirty." He held out his arm. "My chronometer," he said proudly. "Would you like to know the time in Nepal?"

"Um, no thanks, Your Highness."

"Really, my dear," the princess said to me, "you must get some rest if you are no longer hungry. There are so many things to do, and such a short time."

What did she mean? A short time till what?

It must be that I was going to take over the throne pretty soon. Maybe the prince and princess planned to take a retirement trip when she stepped down, and they already had their tickets reserved.

"And you do not have to call us Your Highness. You may call us Mummy."

Both of you? The "us" confused me until I remembered that that was the way royalty referred to their royal persons. When Queen Victoria said, "We are not amused," she was speaking for herself, not a group.

"And you may call us Papa," the prince said.

"Do you think you could call us — I mean, me — Abby? I'm not sure why you're saying I'm Dolores."

"Dolores is your Christian name," said the princess. "Dolores Theodora Marie Celeste."

I shook my head. "This is very confusing. I thought I was Florinda."

"You will be when you ascend to the throne," Mummy explained. "Florinda the Fourteenth. We are Florinda the Thirteenth."

"It's just that I'm so used to being Abby. Couldn't you call your other daughter Dolores, and call me Abby? By the way, I've been wondering about her. I'd really like to meet her."

The prince and princess exchanged worried looks, just like my parents do, right over my head. It must be a universal gesture, used by parents the world over, no matter what their race, color, creed, or national origin.

"Of course," I added, "I understand if you have to call me Dolores for some royal reason. I'll just have to get used to it. But I really would like to meet my —" What was Dolores to me? She was actually my mother's daughter — only my mother wasn't my mother.

"I mean, we're practically twins. It would be nice to have someone my own age to talk to. She can tell me about being a princess and I can tell her about being a commoner. We could be like sisters."

My father, the prince, frowned. My mother, the princess, twiddled the fringe on her shawl.

"Dolores — that is, Abby Adams — is a little perturbed about this whole turn of events," Papa began.

"It was quite traumatic," Mummy said.

Good grief, the shock had destroyed Dolores's mind and they'd chained her up in the dungeon.

"But if we could just get to know each other," I persisted, "I'm sure we'd be friends."

The prince shook his head. "As they say in America," he replied gloomily, "don't bet the farm."

My room was called a chamber. Compared to the chamber, my room at home was a closet. It was so big I might need to carry a water canteen to hike from the bed to the dressing table.

Even with the huge, draped canopy bed, the massive armoire, the chaise longue, the bookcases, the desk, two bedside tables, the oversized dresser, three rugs, and a complicated curtain arrangement at the long, narrow windows, I could have invited twenty friends to dance all night and none of us would have bumped into anything.

There was a fireplace on the wall opposite the bed. From that distance, it looked like a toaster oven.

The bathroom was not nearly as spectacular. I was glad to see that it had all the standard fixtures, but they would have appeared in Chapter One of *The History of Western Plumbing*.

The bathtub had feet — paws, really — with spiky little gold claws. The toilet seemed to have no flush mechanism, till I looked up, and saw there was a chain dangling from the wall behind it.

But.

Someone had prepared a bubble bath for me, and there were big, fluffy white towels piled on a marble-topped table, and my bathrobe was hung on a fancy white iron clothes pole in the middle of the room, even though I hadn't unpacked anything.

Maybe best of all was the grate in the wall which glowed red with heat and warmed up the whole bathroom.

After my bath I discovered that someone had put my clothes in the armoire and the dresser. My stereo sat on the desk, my few books and French dictionary were shelved in the bookcase. The quilt on my bed was turned down. My pajamas were laid out so neatly and precisely that they looked as if they had been cut from a paper doll book.

Even the curtains had been closed, so the evening light wouldn't keep me awake.

The hot bubble bath made me even sleepier than I was when Mummy showed me to my chamber. I was so tired I didn't even bother with my pajamas. I just climbed into bed — and I really did have to climb — in my robe, turned off the little lamp next to me, and pulled the warm, satin quilt up to my ears.

It felt like I was sinking into a giant sea of marshmallows. The bed and the quilt embraced me like a mother's arms.

My mother, I thought sleepily. I should have called home to tell them I'd arrived safely.

I ought to get out of bed right now and go find a phone. They're probably worried about me. And no matter how tired I am, I'll never fall asleep. Not in this vast, imposing room, not in this drafty palace, not in this weird country where everyone wears plastic raincoats and they lock up ex-princesses in the dungeon.

I snuggled into the pillow. It was so comfortable, so absolutely luxurious, that I thought it must be sinful. Or at least fattening.

Gradually I began to realize the significance of all this: the bath, the unpacking, the fire blazing in the fireplace. I didn't have to lift a finger to get any of those things done. All I had to lift were my royal toes into the bathwater, and my royal body into this delicious bed.

Nobody would ever tell me to iron my own shirt if I wanted it ironed.

Nobody would ever tell me, if we were out of, say, shampoo, "Go buy some. The walk will do you good."

*Nobody would ever tell me to clean my room.*

Servants would clean my room.

Laundresses would keep me supplied with ironed shirts.

Shampoo, bubbling bathwater, toasty fires, goat cheese delicacies — all would magically appear whenever I wanted them. A regiment of servants camped in the palace, primed to cater to my every whim, trained to provide me with every comfort, every luxury, everything my royal heart desired.

That's what being a princess means, I thought.

*What a deal.*

When I woke up the next morning, the room was so dark I didn't know it was the next morning.

But I knew exactly where I was. I didn't have that eerie, where-am-I? feeling you read about in books. I knew I was in the princess's royal chamber, and when I pulled my arm out from under the covers, I found that my royal chamber was freezing cold.

The fire in the fireplace had gone out. "Someone will hear about this," I grumbled. I ducked under the covers and wondered what I was supposed to do now.

I didn't know what time it was. If it wasn't so cold, I'd take my arm out from under the cover again and check my watch, but what would that tell me? That would tell me the time in France, which was the last country in which I had reset my watch.

I finally decided that, except for the fact that my blood was freezing in my veins instead of flowing, I felt pretty chipper. Therefore, it couldn't be the middle of the night. I was refreshed and alert, and if my room weren't the temperature of an igloo, I would hop right out of bed and go find something to eat.

Hey! I don't have to go find something to eat, I realized. Somebody will bring me something to eat. All I have to do is contact the person in charge of royal breakfasts.

But how? In a palace this size, it was possible I'd have to send a telegram. In a *room* this size it was possible I'd have to send a telegram.

I twisted around to look for the bellpull. I was not completely ignorant of royal customs. In all the movies I'd ever seen about monarchs, there was always a red velvet rope near the bed to summon the servants.

There was no red velvet rope near the bed. I had to crane my neck to look, because the bedposts were draped with heavy yellow tie-back curtains and the canopy on top went down the wall behind the bed.

I did see an embroidered brocade strip hanging near one of the bedposts, but I hesitated to pull it. I looked up at the elaborate canopy, the thick folds of curtains, and I couldn't tell how anything connected with anything else.

Were all these bed hangings rigged together? I had a sudden terrible conviction that if I pulled that brocade strip, the whole arrangement would collapse and come crashing down on my head, and I'd smother in a sea of marshmallows, damask, and goose feathers.

I sat there for a moment, shivering, as I debated whether or not to pull the dangling end of brocade. A good leader, I told myself finally, has to be able to make the tough decisions.

I yanked the strip of material and dived under the covers, crossing my arms over my head.

Nothing happened. I mean, *nothing*. The canopy didn't come tumbling down, and no servants magically appeared bearing breakfast.

Give it time, I told myself. After all, the kitchen could be two miles from here. My breakfast might arrive by goat cart.

I waited for what seemed an awfully long time. Finally I thought I heard a soft scratching at the door.

"Come in!"

The door inched open, just far enough for someone to peek in.

"Come in, already. I mean, *entrez*."

The door swung open all the way. A girl about my age, with long, straight brown hair, stood in the doorway. She was wearing a dark blue velvet robe with a gold rope sash. She was carrying a fuzzy, stuffed Snoopy.

"Dolores!" I cried. "I'm so glad to meet you. You are Dolores, aren't you? I'm Abby Adams. Is it always so cold here? *Parlez-vous anglais?*"

She didn't *parlez* anything. She just stood there, her head cocked to one side, scrutinizing me. Her dark eyes narrowed. I told myself that it wasn't that she didn't like me. She was just squinting because of the distance from the door to the bed.

Why is she staring like that? I wondered. Why isn't she answering me? Why doesn't she say something?

Why is she carrying a Snoopy doll?

She raised Snoopy level with her chest, like she was displaying it to me. I looked into the dog's beady black eyes and coughed nervously. I got the eerie feeling that *I* was being displayed to the *doll*.

"There she is, Snoopy," the girl said finally. I nearly jumped. "You're the one who wanted to see her. Are you satisfied now?"

Oh, brother. Had Dolores always been dippy, or did she only slip into the Outer Limits when she was deprincessed? This girl made me very tense. She might be dangerous.

Chaining her up in the dungeon began to sound like a good idea.

"You speak English." I tried to sound cheery and unthreatening. "I'm so glad. I wanted to —"

"You are right, Snoopy," she said loudly. "The American is not very interesting at all. We will watch the morning exercise program on television."

She turned on her heel and I heard her slippers flip-flopping as she padded down the hall.

"Yeeks," I said, and hopped out of bed to close the door.

I shivered as I trekked to the armoire to get some

warm clothes, and it wasn't just because of the arctic climate in my chamber.

Maybe it used to be *her* chamber, I thought, as I pulled on jeans and socks and legwarmers. Maybe they kicked her out of here when they found out she wasn't the real princess.

I could certainly understand why this whole business would make her a bit hostile toward me. After all, it can't be pleasant to be deprincessed — or dethroned, or decastled, or whatever it is you call a defrocked princess.

I pulled on a wool sweater and a sweat shirt. I wrapped a scarf around my neck. The prince had tried to warn me that Dolores might be somewhat unfriendly, but I certainly wasn't prepared for an ex-princess who was not only unfriendly, but loony tunes.

I laced up my sneakers. My fingers felt like icicles. Maybe downstairs, at a lower altitude, the temperature was higher, but I wasn't taking any chances. I pulled on my red mittens and silently thanked my mother for insisting that I bring along some warm clothing.

Even though I'd only been awake for about fifteen minutes, and even though Dolores the Deranged had only said a few words, I'd learned some important things already.

Number One: It definitely was morning.

Number Two: Saxony Coburn had television.

Number Three: I had a dangerous enemy in the palace, who, now that she had no royal obligations to fulfill, could spend hours plotting against me with the aid of her stuffed accomplice.

It was hard to imagine Snoopy — of all creatures — as an enemy, but no matter how hungry I felt, someone was going to taste my goat-cheese omelet before I ate it.

"There you are, my dear!" The prince smiled, but I could see his eyes travel curiously from my sneakers, past my legwarmers to my red turtleneck, purple sweat shirt, and blue scarf. He lingered awhile on my cherry-red mittens.

"What style the Americans have!" he exclaimed. "Don't you think so, my sweet?"

The princess seemed mesmerized by my mittens. "Mmm," she said. "But we can fix that."

"I was cold," I said. "Isn't it spring here yet?"

"It is still chilly in the mornings," said Papa. "This old building retains the night air."

The prince and princess sat at a table in a small dining room in the Moorish wing of the palace. I'd managed to find my way with the help of two servants who bowed and fluttered and spoke only French.

"I could eat a goat," I hinted. I wasn't sure I was supposed to sit down unless they invited me.

"Chow down," Papa said heartily.

"Yes, dear, do," Mummy urged. "You will have a very busy day. Did you sleep well?"

"Yes, thank you. Only, it was very cold in my room when I woke up. The fire went out. And the bellpull didn't work." And I met your dippy daughter. . . .

I gazed hungrily at the breakfast table. Bacon, eggs, sausages, bread, rolls, toast, a bowl of something hot and mushy, fruit — and next to the prince's place setting, a box of Cap'n Crunch.

"I didn't know you could get Cap'n Crunch here."

I piled bacon and eggs and rolls and sausages and toast and a banana on my plate.

"We import it," the princess said. "Albert does love his Cap'n Crunch. Now, dear, we are glad you're well-rested. We have much to do in a very short time. We have had to double up on some things. You will be in quite a whirl before this week is over."

There she goes again, talking about how little time there is. How little time till what? What was the big rush?

"As soon as you have eaten, we will meet with the dressmaker. She will start work on your ball gown right away." She glanced at my mittens. "You will need some daytime clothes, too."

That must be the reason for the rush. There was a ball next week. How exciting! I wondered when the shoemaker would come to measure me for my glass slippers.

"While you are being fitted, M. Creanga will begin your etiquette and protocol lessons."

Etiquette? I checked my place setting. I was eating with a fork, my napkin was in my lap, and I was chewing with my mouth closed.

She probably means princess etiquette, I decided. How to christen ships, read proclamations, stuff like that.

"Then Madame Banat, your tutor, will work with you on French and the history of our country. Do you speak any French?"

"A little. *Un peu.* I have to call my — um — *mère* and *père*."

"We sent a telegram to your . . . adoptive parents last night. We will have our secretary call them for you, if you wish. It may take some time. But, my dear, *we* are your mother and father. It would make us very happy if you would think of us as Mummy."

"And Papa," the prince added.

"I'll try," I said. "I just have to get used to it." Would I ever get used to thinking of the prince and princess as Mummy and Daddy?

"I'd really like it," I said carefully, "if you'd call me Abby, though, instead of Dolores. I met Dolores this morning and she seemed —"

They looked startled. "You met her? How?" the princess asked.

"She came into my room. She seemed sort of . . . odd. She wouldn't talk to me." I didn't mention that she talked to a plush animal. I was sure they knew that already.

"Dolores hasn't been herself these days," the prince said sadly.

How could she be? She was *me* now.

"She took the news very hard," the princess said. "She won't talk to anybody except Snoopy."

"If she's really my mother's — I mean, my American mother's daughter, why doesn't she go live with them in Kansas?" Not that I would wish Dolores on my family, but my parents ought to be eager to meet their real daughter.

"We suggested an exchange," Papa said. "Not that we were anxious to give her up. After all, we have always thought of her as our daughter. But your mother was entitled to have her child back. Dolores refused."

Mummy nodded. "And we certainly wouldn't force her to leave the only home she's ever known, and the only way of life she's ever lived. The adjustment would have been too difficult."

They couldn't force *her*, but they could force me. They didn't worry about how difficult *my* adjustment would be.

Well, maybe that was to be expected. After all, I was an important personage in Saxony Coburn. *Noblesse oblige* — the responsibility of noble people. They needed me here. Whereas Kansas could manage very well without Dolores.

And it was probably true that she would never adjust to being a commoner. If she was unhinged because she wasn't a princess anymore, she'd keel over the first time my mother told her to iron her own shirt.

That meant I was stuck with her. A bitter, possibly deranged rival, with every reason to hate me and plenty of opportunities to do something about it.

"Are you sure she's . . . all right?" I asked nervously.

"Oh, yes," Mummy assured me. "The doctor said it was just a temporary refusal to accept the situation. She is trying to cling to her happy childhood. He is not alarmed."

Why should the doctor be alarmed? Dolores wasn't going to poison *his* goat-cheese omelet.

"She will get over it," the princess said. "Now, if you are finished eating, we must get started." She consulted a small, leather-bound notebook. "After your lessons you will be taken on a tour of the palace. You will meet the staff, and learn about our daily schedules, and. . . ."

The list of things I had to do went on and on. It seemed that the life of a princess was not all bubble baths and featherbeds.

" . . . dancing lessons, learn the national anthem, pose for your postage stamp. . . . Not all today, of course, but. . . ."

My stamp! Me, on a stamp! I wished I could see Teddy's face when he got his first letter from me.

"And call America," I remembered. "May we do that first — um — Mummy?"

"A hoopskirt?" I said. "She's going to make me a gown with a hoopskirt?" I nearly fell off the dressmaker's stool.

"With layer upon layer of fluffy ruffles," Mummy said dreamily.

It sounded like my gown was going to be made of potato chips.

"But hoopskirts went out with the Civil War!" I wailed.

"Which one?" asked the princess.

Mlle Chenille eyed me nervously. She looked at the princess. *"La princesse est distraite?"*

*"La princesse* is very *distraite!"* I said. "I'm not the hoopskirt-and-ruffles type. Really, I'm not. Couldn't

I have something more up-to-date?"

"You'll look just like Princess Grace did in *The Swan*." Mummy closed her eyes, as if she was visualizing Princess Grace in *The Swan*. I'd never heard of it, but I assumed it was an old movie.

"*Soyez tranquille*, Chenille," Mummy said. "*La princesse est fatiguée.*"

M. Creanga cleared his throat. "If I may continue, Your Highness?"

"*Oui, oui, continuez,*" said the princess.

*Fatiguée* was right. I'd been standing on that stool for over an hour, with the dressmaker fussing and bustling around me, turning me in every direction, and occasionally jabbing me with a pin in some unexpected part of my anatomy.

I was wrapped in about two hundred yards of muslin and I had no idea how I was ever going to get out of the stuff. I thought I might have to wear it all week, while Mlle Chenille constructed the ball gown around it day by day.

Meanwhile, M. Creanga was trying to teach me how to act like a princess in public, and Mummy kept running in and out of the sewing room every ten minutes to confer with her secretary and to add new things to the list of what I had to do this week.

I was *fatiguée*d just thinking of all the things I still had to do today. And my phone call to America hadn't come through yet.

"Of course, we don't expect you to know all the correct forms of address," M. Creanga was saying, "but if you listen very carefully as each person is introduced, the title will be included in the presentation. If I say, 'His Excellency, the Prime Minister of Eritrea,' you will call him 'Your Excellency.' "

"You'll say it in English? I'll never get it right if you say it in French."

"We'll say it in both languages. Now, the gentlemen will either kiss your hand, or bow."

"Hey, neat. I've never had my hand kissed."

M. Creanga cleared his throat again. "It would be inappropriate, Mademoiselle, if you appeared to enjoy it. In any case, the kiss is simply a formal touch of the lips to the hand."

"You mean, no slobbering, right?"

"Your Highness," he said firmly, "many of the people on the receiving line will be royalty themselves. Royalty does not slobber."

"OW!"

Mlle Chenille pardoned herself a million times and gestured for me to get down off the stool. As the muslin moved, I felt little pinpricks all over my legs and shoulders.

The sewing room door opened and a young woman in a white blouse and a severe black skirt entered, carrying a load of books and papers.

She smiled. "Ahh. My princess. My pupil." She curtseyed gracefully, in spite of her narrow skirt and armful of books.

I liked her right away. She seemed so glad to meet me.

"You acknowledge the curtsey with a cordial nod of the head," M. Creanga said.

I smiled and nodded enthusiastically.

"Not quite so cordial, Your Highness. A slight inclination of the head will do."

"You must be my tutor," I said.

"That is my pleasure and my privilege," the woman replied.

"Madame Banat," M. Creanga said.

I could almost feel the dressmaker seething with impatience behind me.

*"Beaucoup de choses, pas assez de temps,"* Mme Banat said. "So much to do, so little time. We'll start your lessons immediately. *Nous commencerons vos leçons tout de suite."*

Mlle Chenille shrieked. I whirled around just in time to see her kick a bolt of taffeta halfway across the room. She stomped around the stool and began screaming and sobbing in French.

"Was it something I said?" asked Mme Banat innocently.

*"Quatre jours!"* Mlle Chenille cried. *"Quatre jours pour une robe de soirée pour une princesse. Je suis artiste, pas automaton!"*

"Four days to make a ball gown for a princess," Mme Banat translated. "I'm an artist, not a robot."

"I figured it out," I said.

"And you respond the same way to a man," M. Creanga droned on relentlessly. "A gracious but impersonal nod of the head."

Mlle Chenille grabbed at the muslin wildly, still babbling in brokenhearted French.

"OW!" Every time she pointed or pushed at the muslin I got jabbed with pins.

"Two suits, two dresses, evening wrap." Mme Banat continued translating the dressmaker's frustration.

I wanted to scream, myself. And throw my hands over my ears. This was crazy. "OW!"

The door opened again and another woman came in. She had a large notebook opened against her chest.

"Mlle Grusk," M. Creanga introduced her. "Your mother's secretary."

Mlle Grusk curtsied. I acknowledged her curtsey with a gracious but impersonal nod of the head.

"Good," said M. Creanga.

"Ahh, *comme elle est belle*," the secretary sighed. *"Je suis folle de joie. . . .* Oh. You have a telephone call."

"Telephone call!" I hiked up the two hundred yards of my muslin skirt a little so I could move, and raced, barefooted, toward the door.

Mlle Chenille screamed one last, horrible time. She threw her arms up in the air. Thousands of pins shot out of her hands and rained down all over the place.

"Ow, ooh, ouch, ooh, ooh!" The floor was littered with pins.

"Where's the telephone?" I demanded, and practically dragged Mlle Grusk out of the room.

It was wonderful to talk to my (American) family. My parents told me they were packing my trunk and would send it off tomorrow.

"Don't forget my roller skates," I said. "This place is so big I might need them to get from room to room."

Teddy asked if I had to wear a crown all the time.

As soon as I hung up the phone, a wave of homesickness hit me.

I followed listlessly as M. Creanga, Mme Banat, and Mlle Grusk led me on a tour of the palace. Mlle Grusk gave me a map to check as we hiked from room to room. I couldn't help thinking of my extremely ordinary home in Kansas. I didn't need a map to find my way to the kitchen there.

"Every Tuesday and Thursday the ground floor is open for guided tours. Please remain out of that area between one and three o'clock."

"When am I ever going to see anybody?" We were in the Gothic wing of the palace, and portraits of the first thirteen Florindas stared at me from the walls of the portrait gallery. I felt empty and lonely and tired and cold. Mlle Chenille had confiscated my mittens, and I had no friends here.

"You will meet people suitable to your station," M. Creanga said.

"Why, only this Saturday, at your grand ball," Mlle Grusk said, "you will meet many people from fine, noble families. And once you meet your betrothed, you'll —"

"My *what*?"

"Your betrothed," she repeated. "Prince Casimir Clovis Fabian Alaric of Arcania."

"But what does that mean, betrothed?" I asked.

Mme Banat looked sort of uncomfortable, as if I wanted her to explain where babies come from.

"It means engaged," she said. "You've been engaged to Prince Casimir since you were seven years old."

## 8

Finding out you're betrothed to a prince you've never met, from a country you've never heard of, is an effective way to clear your mind of other trivial matters. But it does raise a few important questions.

Like, *"Are you kidding?"*

Nobody answered me. All of a sudden everybody wanted to hustle me back to the family quarters, because it was ten to one, and the common folk would be wandering around the palace any minute now. The royal portrait gallery, where the thirteen Florindas hung, was part of the tour.

"Okay. Fine. Let me see the prince and princess.

There are a few things I want to know about this betrothed business."

Unfortunately, seeing my parents wasn't on my schedule. Fortunately, lunch was. The meal was laid out on a table in an upstairs dining room. M. Creanga and Mme Banat sat with me. They kept drilling me on how to be a princess and the history of Saxony Coburn.

Even though I was starving, I waited for my drill team to start eating before I would taste anything, just to make sure that neither of them keeled over into the soup.

But they didn't eat. They didn't even lift their spoons.

My suspicions were right, I thought morbidly. They're afraid Dolores is going to poison the food, too.

I wondered how I'd ever be able to carry out the duties of my office without the aid and support of the calories I loved.

"Isn't Your Highness hungry?" M. Creanga finally asked.

"Actually, I'm . . . uh . . . waiting for you to start."

M. Creanga looked startled. "But, Your Highness, we cannot eat until you begin."

"Ohh." No wonder we were all sitting there not eating.

"Does Dolores hang out in the kitchen much?" I tried to sound casual. "Look, I don't want you to think I'm paranoid or anything, but I met her this morning and she hated me on sight. She's a little weird. I mean, the girl talks to her Snoopy. And Snoopy doesn't like me, either."

"I do not think," M. Creanga said, "that you have anything to fear from Dolores. Or her doll," he added.

"I just have this feeling they're plotting against me. They make me nervous."

"There's no reason to be nervous," Mme Banat assured me. "Dolores is only sulking. She is used to getting her own way."

"They don't keep any arsenic around here, do they?"

"You're afraid Dolores will try to poison you?" she asked, astonished. "Is that why you won't eat?"

I nodded. "Then she could be rethroned, once she got rid of me."

"You are waiting," M. Creanga said, "for us to taste your food?"

I nodded again. I was beginning to feel a little silly.

Mme Banat didn't hesitate another instant. She took a spoonful of every dish that was on the table, arranged the little piles on her plate, and tasted every one of them.

"You see, Your Highness, I am not dead. Now please eat. You will need your strength."

She ladled some soup into a bowl for me. I studied her carefully. Her hand didn't shake, her face wasn't ashen, and she didn't clutch her throat and slump over into the tureen.

That was reassuring.

"Okay," I said finally. "Chow down."

I felt better after lunch. And Mme Banat was right. The way I was being dragged around from one thing to another made me grateful that I had stocked up on those 3,700 calories.

I had a thousand questions to ask, all of them about my betrothal, but nobody was answering them. "No time now; can't slow down. Later." I felt like Alice trying to keep up with the Red Queen.

Mlle Chenille did more fittings after lunch. Her sketches for my outfits were totally depressing. The designs ran the gamut from dull to dowdy. I wondered if I'd ever get out of the palace long enough to buy a few zippy accessories to perk up the tailored navy blue suit and flat beige skirts and blouses.

I remembered how the princess had reacted to my clothes this morning, and how Mlle Chenille swiped my mittens. Even if I did find a place in Saxony Coburn that sold zippy accessories, Mummy and the royal dressmaker were sure to zap my zip.

At three o'clock, after the tourists left, my keepers whisked me downstairs to the reception foyer, where the entire palace staff was lined up to meet me.

The line seemed endless.

"The chef . . . the assistant chef . . . the second assistant chef. . . ." Maids, footmen, chauffeurs, gardeners, housekeepers (palacekeepers), the switchboard operator — on and on we went.

Everyone bowed or curtseyed to me. I acknowledged the introductions with a gracious nod of the head.

M. Creanga seemed pleased, until, finally, Mlle Grusk presented my personal maid, Jeannot.

"I have a personal maid?" I exclaimed. "Yippee!"

M. Creanga winced.

"It must have been you who did my bath and everything last night," I said to Jeannot. "Hey, thanks a lot. That was great."

Jeannot was very young. In fact, I thought she was hardly any older than I was. Someone to talk to! Someone to tell me what's what. We can be friends, and she'll know all about this Prince Casimir, and she'll show me where the bellpull is and bring me breakfast in bed. . . .

She curtseyed. I completely forgot my protocol lessons. I reached out and took her hand. I pumped it up and down.

"Nice to meet you, Jeannot," I said excitedly. "Do you speak English?"

*"Oui,"* she said. "But not very."

I patted her hand. "We'll manage," I said. "That's just the way I speak French."

My mind was beginning to overload as we started back upstairs, me and my entourage, which now included Jeannot. Suddenly Mlle Grusk cried, "Oh! The reporter! He's waiting for the princess in the morning room. Jeannot, help the princess change —"

"I have to see a reporter now?"

"Yes, Mademoiselle, for the interview."

I snapped. I'd been surrounded by people poking me with pins, jabbering at me in French and English. I'd trudged for miles through the palace, and hadn't sat down all day, except for breakfast and lunch.

I put my royal foot down. Actually, I stamped it.

"I'm tired!" I shouted. "I'm hungry. I'm cold! I want to rest. I want to watch TV. I want to go outside and see if there's still weather. I want five minutes of peace and quiet with nobody ordering me around. I'm the princess. I should be ordering *you* around!"

I burst into tears.

Everyone fussed about me anxiously, murmuring soothing words and pleas for cooperation.

"It's very important that you speak to the newspaperman as soon as possible," M. Creanga said.

"Why? Why can't it wait until tomorrow?"

"Just this short interview," he urged, "and you will have the rest of the day to yourself."

"What rest of the day?" I grumbled. "The day's practically over."

"It would be a shame," Mme Banat said, "to disappoint that nice, young man."

My ears pricked up.

Nice? Young? Man?

How nice? How young?

Now, Abby, I told myself, mustn't forget you're betrothed.

"And you can do the interview outside," she went on. "You'll get some fresh air, and you can stroll around the grounds."

"I feel this sudden surge of energy," I said. "Come on, Jeannot, let's get dressed."

## 9

Geoffrey Torunga bowed.

He straightened up and I gazed into his deep blue eyes and forgot I was betrothed.

He carried a camera and a small notebook and he looked like a member of the Olympic Downhill Ski Team. To be perfectly honest, he looked like a member of the Olympic Gorgeous Team. Blond division.

I forgot my royal manners.

"It is an honor to meet you, Your Highness," he said, in a soft, deep, sincere voice.

"Yeah."

He didn't kiss my hand, which was just as well,

because I would have enjoyed it, and M. Creanga would have given me ten demerits for failing hand-kissing.

"I can't wait to get outside," I said weakly. The prospect of being alone, in some remote, romantic nook in the royal gardens, where Geoffrey would toss aside his notebook and I would forget my protocol lessons. . . .

" . . . will accompany you."

"What?" I hadn't heard what M. Creanga was saying. I gazed at Geoffrey and tried to picture him without his notebook.

"The princess is always escorted," Mme Banat said. She drew me aside. "M. Creanga wants to make sure that the interview goes well," she whispered.

It would go a lot better if M. Creanga left us alone.

"You mean, I'm not allowed to go anyplace without a chaperone?"

"With a man, you will always be accompanied. Except with Prince Casimir, of course."

"That's awful! I don't want to be followed around all the time and spied on. Besides, what about my right to privacy?"

"You don't have any, Your Highness."

" . . . and what was your reaction when you learned that you were Princess Florinda the Fourteenth?" Geoffrey asked.

"It blew my mind."

He grinned. "Do you want me to quote you?"

I smiled back.

I don't know why we needed M. Creanga's help. Geoffrey was doing just fine. He certainly didn't seem like some of those reporters you see on TV, trying to get people to say embarrassing things about themselves, or asking victims of floods and fires dumb questions like, "How does it feel to lose everything you own and know that it can never be replaced even if you *had* been insured?"

M. Creanga didn't have to coach me at all. Geoffrey made all the suggestions for rephrasing my answers.

It was warmer outside than it was in the palace and the air was springlike. The grounds were beautiful, even though some of the flowers were only beginning to bud.

There was a formal garden and several small wild flower beds. Acres and acres of grass made a vast, green carpet. Stone benches and marble statues dotted the lawns, and tall old trees would provide shade in the summer.

It was so romantic. Just like in the movies. Now, if only M. Creanga would be suddenly called away on important state business.

We sat down to rest on a stone bench near a birdbath.

"So," I said to Geoffrey, "tell me about you."

Oops.

Geoffrey lowered his eyes. I don't think I was supposed to ask him personal questions. M. Creanga frowned.

"The people are not interested in me," Geoffrey said. "They are interested in you, Your Highness."

*I'm* interested in you.

His hair shone like gold in the sun. He scribbled

something in his notebook. "How does Her Highness like her homeland?"

"I haven't seen anything of it yet. I wish I could. I've been cooped up in the palace —" I stopped myself as Geoffrey looked up from his notebook and into my eyes.

Our eyes locked, just for a moment. I thought my heart would stop. M. Creanga started to say something, and we both quickly looked away.

"The princess will be making some public appearances this week. She will visit the plastic raincoat factory and the primary school and will appear on *Good Morning, Saxony Coburn*."

Geoffrey just kept on taking notes. He didn't look at me. It was as if he was afraid to.

"Is that on TV?" I asked. M. Creanga nodded.

"Gee. I've never been on television."

Geoffrey finally looked up from his notebook. "May I have the princess's schedule for the week?" His voice sounded sort of strained. "The newspaper will want coverage."

"Mlle Grusk will keep you informed," M. Creanga said.

And if she doesn't, I will. I was already plotting evasive tactics to elude my chaperones.

"I think I have all I need." Geoffrey closed his notebook.

"Oh, don't go! I'd like to talk to you. You speak English so well. How did you learn?"

"I spent two years at a university in the United States, Your Highness. I was there on a ski scholarship."

I knew it, I knew it! A downhill racer.

"Great. You can tell me about the difference between America and here."

"If Your Highness wishes."

It was as simple as that! *Her Highness wishes.* Magic words. People had to obey me. I was the princess.

What if I said, "Her Highness wishes you to kiss her, you great big hunk, you"? Obviously, Geoffrey, who was a commoner, couldn't come on to a princess — especially a betrothed one. I might have to make the first move.

We started walking back toward the palace. M. Creanga hovered at my side like a nervous butterfly.

"No offense," I said to him, "but please walk twenty feet behind us."

He hesitated.

"Give me a break," I muttered. "All I want is a little normal conversation."

"All the princess's comments will be off the record," he said to Geoffrey.

"Of course."

"All right, Your Highness." But he looked doubtful. And he only gave us ten feet.

"Thank goodness," I sighed. "Now, tell me about yourself. It's so nice to be with someone near my own age. How near my own age are you?"

"Twenty."

A little old, but near enough.

"Did you like it in America? Where did you go to college? I live in Kansas. What do you think about American girls? Do you have a girl friend here?"

I shot questions at him so fast he didn't have a chance to answer any of them.

"Your Highness, please!" He laughed. "One question at a time. Which should I answer first?"

I looked at him curiously. "You know, you seem a lot more relaxed with M. Creanga ten feet behind us." Actually M. Creanga had sneaked up a few feet when Geoffrey laughed, but I shot him a stern look and he dropped back again.

"I hope I'm not making you uncomfortable or anything," I said. "I guess I'm asking a lot of personal questions, but I'm really interested."

"You can ask me as many personal questions as you like," he replied. He paused a moment. "But I can't ask you any — no matter how interested I am."

I wasn't imagining things. He'd fallen in love with me the instant we looked into each other's eyes.

Could that happen? Was love at first sight really possible?

Well, two days ago I was studying for finals in Kansas and here I was, Princess Florinda XIV of Saxony Coburn. If that could happen, anything was possible.

My heart started to pound so hard I thought it might burst through my sweater.

"Go ahead," I said shakily. "You can ask me anything you — yikes!"

Suddenly my foot hit something in the grass, and I stumbled. I fell against Geoffrey and he caught me in his arms. I clung to him till I got my balance — maybe a few seconds longer.

M. Creanga rushed toward us and Geoffrey let go of me. He was still holding his camera, but his notebook was lying on the grass.

Our eyes locked again, and a jolt of electricity passed between us, like we both realized how we felt at the same time.

Geoffrey stooped down to pick up his notebook as M. Creanga took my arm.

"No problem, no problem," I said weakly.

"You must be careful of the underground sprinkler jets," M. Creanga warned. "You're sure you haven't injured yourself?"

"I'm fine." *I'm not fine.* Get back behind us where you belong. If I'm lucky, I'll trip over another sprinkler.

"You're sure you're okay?" Geoffrey asked when we were out of hearing range.

"I think so."

I tried to get a grip on myself. But my heart was hammering and I felt dizzy and lightheaded. I knew I was overtired. I knew I was lonely and vulnerable.

I knew I was betrothed.

I also knew that I'd just fallen — probably hopelessly — in love with the most gorgeous commoner I'd ever seen in my life.

# 10

*Friday*

Dear Carol,

*Guess what? I'm betrothed. To a prince. Guess what else? I'm in love with a commoner. He's the reporter who came to interview me. . . .*

I put down my pen and shook my head helplessly. How could I possibly tell Carol all that had gone on this week in a letter? I had to talk to her.

The only thing was, for some reason, it was never the right time for a phone call. Either there was no room on my schedule for it, or I had to wait until the long distance rates went down, when it would be the middle of the night in America, and I didn't want to wake my friend, did I?

Why the princess of Saxony Coburn could only call the U.S. at bargain rates was a mystery to me. At first, still thinking of plots and palace intrigue and Dippy Dolores, I was suspicious that the prince and princess were trying to keep me from contacting the outside world.

But that didn't make much sense. I finally decided that the royal family might not be as rich as I thought.

I mean, there were only two television sets in the whole palace, and no VCRs. Sure, there were six-course lunches and tea, and Mlle Chenille, sewing her nimble fingers into nubs for a lavish — and ridiculous — ball gown, not to mention a daytime wardrobe. But the place didn't have central heating, half of the rooms had no furniture, and I saw M. Blitzen counting up the money after Thursday's public visiting hours. (Admission: 2 zelwigs.)

I started to rip up the letter to Carol, but the elegant palace stationery was too expensive to rip up. It was creamy white, with the coat of arms of Saxony Coburn at the top: a purple gloxinia on a white shield with *In Florinda Veritas* printed in purple raised italics underneath.

So I just folded it up and stuck it in my desk.

It was so nice to have an hour to myself after a whirlwind week of public appearances, constant instruction, bouts of homesickness, and the strain of trying to talk like a princess instead of like me.

It was exciting and all that, and some of the instruction was very valuable. I learned that to ring for Jeannot and get breakfast in bed, all I had to do was to dial the phone on my desk. It was an in-palace intercom system. But the thing that kept me going was that I saw Geoffrey at every ceremonial appearance I made.

When the workers presented me with a custom-made plastic raincoat with the Saxony Coburn coat of arms stamped on the back, Geoffrey was right there at the plastic raincoat factory, taking notes.

When I was interviewed on *Good Morning, Saxony Coburn*, Geoffrey stood behind the cameraman, snapping photos of me being televised.

Being on television was pretty exciting, even if it wasn't exactly *The Tonight Show*. Everyone said I looked very pretty and did a fine job, though I was a little flustered when the show's hostess curtseyed as she introduced me.

I got a kick out of seeing my pictures in the Saxony Coburn newspaper. *La Journée* was in French, but Mme Banat helped me read about myself every morning as part of my French lessons.

The days went by in a blur. No one explained anything about my betrothal, no matter how often I asked. I was kept so busy that most of the time I was too tired to remember to ask.

But tomorrow was the ball. I'd find everything out at the ball.

I turned on the little black and white TV set that Papa had given me.

I leaned back in the chaise longue. *The Mouse That Roared* was on the eight o'clock movie. It was in French, but I'd seen it before, so I knew when to laugh. Mme Banat encouraged TV watching. She said that would help with my French, also.

The door to my chamber was open and I didn't hear anyone come in, but as I watched the movie I suddenly had the strangest feeling that someone was watching *me*.

I looked up. Dolores was standing next to my bed. She was holding Snoopy. They were both staring at me.

I felt a cold shiver down my spine.

"Hi, Dolores. Want to watch television with me?"

For a moment she didn't say anything. Then, softly, she began to talk to her doll.

"She is going to the ball tomorrow, Snoopy. Everybody will be there, except you and me. They will announce her betrothal to Prince Casimir. Prince Casimir will not like her. He loves me.

"But he will marry her anyway and they will live in the palace. She will be the princess and I will marry a factory worker and live in a hut and milk the goat."

She talked so softly and the room was so large, that I had to strain my ears to hear what she was saying. I hardly breathed as I listened, and I started to get goose bumps — even though the royal housekeeper had put an electric heater in my room.

*Spooky.* All right, she wouldn't poison my food, but she sure wasn't the type of person you'd want creeping into your room in the middle of the night.

"Hey, listen, Dolores," I said, "you can come to the ball. Snoopy, too. Why not? You'll be my special guest. Er, guests. And I'll bet you're right. I'll bet the prince won't like me at all. That's okay. I don't mind. I know he loves you. He'll probably insist on marrying you instead of me. Hey — *n-o-o-o* problem. He's a prince. He can do what he wants."

She didn't look at me as I chattered away, but she didn't ignore me.

"Isn't she stupid, Snoopy? She knows nothing about real life, does she? Poor Casimir. He needs a throne. Poor Mummy and Papa. They need his money. Poor Saxony Coburn. They get stuck with *her*."

She sighed deeply and tucked her dog under her arm. She started toward the door.

"No, Dolores, wait! Wait a minute, don't go."

"And she thinks I could go to the ball." Dolores spoke a little louder, like she wanted to make sure I heard her. "After the scandal she caused! I'll be lucky if I can show my face in public ever again."

She padded out of the room as silently as she had come in.

I was right! The royal family was broke. They were marrying me off to Prince Casimir for his money.

I was so shocked I couldn't move a muscle.

Our betrothal would be officially announced tomorrow night. Did they believe in long engagements here, or what? Just how soon did they need the cash?

Probably *soon*. That's why everyone was so evasive whenever I asked questions. That's why the prince and princess wouldn't talk about Casimir with me. *Nobody wanted me to know.*

Scandal I remembered. M. Creanga had said something about a scandal, too, hadn't he? I just couldn't remember when he said it.

I hiked to the desk and dialed my royal parents' chambers.

"This is the princess. I want to speak to the princess."

"I much regret, Your Highness, the prince and princess have retired for the evening."

"At eight-thirty? Well, they can't be asleep yet. I want to speak to one of them. *Now*."

The voice started babbling in rapid-fire French. (A pretty sneaky trick, I thought.) All I understood was, *"Je regrette, je regrette."*

"All right, all right, enough. I know when I'm licked. But if they're asleep, what are *you* doing there?"

I can wait one more day, I told myself. I'll have breakfast with the prince and princess tomorrow, and if I don't get anything out of them then, I'll find out by tomorrow night. They can't very well hold their hands over my ears when they announce my engagement.

And on Sunday I'd phone Kansas.

I turned up the TV again.

Saxony Coburn only had one station, but by some freak of weather, we pulled in Bulgarian TV. It was pretty dull — mostly all you saw were folk dancers or people driving tractors.

But I'd missed half an hour of the movie already, and I wasn't in a laughing mood anymore, so I switched to the Bulgarian channel.

Some sort of variety show was on. A man finished a song, and after the applause an emcee introduced the next act.

It was a bunch of folk dancers.

# 11

"Your Highness, I have the honor of presenting His Royal Highness, Prince Casimir Clovis Fabian Alaric, heir to the throne of Arcania."

Very tall. Very thin. Very handsome.

No electricity.

I held out my hand, which was trembling. He snapped his heels together, bowed from the waist, and smacked his lips over my glove.

I tried to get my hand back.

So, nobility doesn't slobber, eh?

The prince clasped my hand in both of his, and pressed all three hands against his chest, which was covered with gleaming medals.

"My bride," he said.

"Not yet," I said.

M. Creanga cleared his throat. "Your Highness," he said to Casimir, "we would be pleased if you would stand in the receiving line next to the princess. I'm sure our guests would be honored to greet you."

"We will be at her side eternally," he replied, and did a crisp about-face to stand on my left.

I'll bet he said the same thing to Dolores two weeks ago.

M. Creanga leaned down to whisper in my ear. "Please, Your Highness, remember your protocol."

I nodded. I hadn't done very well on my first introduction, but I couldn't help it. I was so nervous, and hearing this tall, dark stranger call me his bride the minute he saw me rattled me even more.

Now that Prince Casimir wasn't slobbering over my hand anymore, the line began to move. M. Blitzen stood on one end of the receiving line with the prince and princess next to him. M. Creanga stood on my right, so he could introduce me to each guest.

I peered around the glittering ballroom to look for Geoffrey. I was sure he was here. This was big time stuff. One hundred and fifty noblepersons, including kings and queens of countries I'd never heard of, and princes of countries that didn't have princes anymore — Geoffrey's newspaper wouldn't want to miss all those photo opportunities. Not to mention the announcement of my betrothal.

If the royal family was broke, you'd never know it from this bash. The ballroom glowed with the light from crystal chandeliers. The chairs lined up against the walls were covered with blue satin. The refreshment table was half the length of a football field.

They must have charged everything on their Saxony Coburn Express Card. By the time the bills rolled in, Casimir's money might be rolling in, too.

While I searched for Geoffrey, my betrothed whispered extravagant compliments into my ear, which was very distracting. I didn't like the way his breath felt on my ear.

I mean, let's face it. It was instant dislike. I don't know why — maybe because of the way he tried to chew my glove — but right away I got the feeling that this Casimir was a royal creep.

"You are magnificent," he declared. "You look like the bride on a wedding cake."

"You think so?" I said indifferently. "The dressmaker ran out of the room in hysterics when I told her what I thought of this gown."

If he really liked this mass of ruffles, ribbons, and hoops, he had lousy taste.

"The Count and Countess Frumelle, of Avignon," M. Creanga announced. I nodded graciously and held out my hand.

"No family, great wealth," Casimir whispered. "Pretentious upstarts."

"Speaking of pretentious upstarts, where is Arcania anyway?"

"Ho, ho," the prince said. "We love that brash American wit. My kingdom is in Constantinople."

"You mean Istanbul?"

"No, Constantinople. Formerly Byzantium." He scowled.

This was a little confusing, but since Prince Casimir was obviously touchy about it, I didn't press the issue.

At last I spotted Geoffrey. He stood at the entrance to the ballroom, snapping pictures and taking notes as the guests entered.

He was wearing formal clothes: white jacket, white tie, black pants with a satin stripe down the side. He looked absolutely spectacular.

I guess it would be sort of tacky if he wandered around the ballroom in a trench coat and slouch hat. This way, except for his camera and notebook, he looked just like a guest.

Geoffrey, I thought, look at me. You know where I am. Just turn around and look at me. Maybe I can get through this if I can see that you love me.

But he didn't turn around, and what good would it do if he did? Our love was hopeless, and getting hopelesser by the minute. Any time now he would hear the official announcement that I was to be married to this tall, dark, handsome drip standing next to me.

Geoffrey was too proper to do anything that would compromise my honor.

Finally the last guest trickled down the receiving line. What a relief. My feet hurt, my back hurt, and my glove felt tight, as if my hand had swollen from all the kissing.

Geoffrey moved away from the door, and turned in my direction at last. He was too far away for me to read the look in his eyes, but he looked at me and Prince Casimir for a long moment.

I nodded my head slowly, hoping he understood that I was trying to signal hello to him, and not just doing neck relaxation exercises.

My knees felt a little watery, and it wasn't because I'd been standing for an hour and a half.

"When is the announcement?" I asked M. Creanga.

"Just before supper."

"When is supper?"

"After the dancing."

"*All right*," I said impatiently, "when is the dancing?"

My father, the prince, stepped forward. He pointed to the band, which was down at the other end of the room. "Hit it, Lester!" he cried. "Come on, everybody, let's boogie!"

I was trying to figure out how you could boogie to *The Blue Danube Waltz*, which is what Lester hit, when Prince Casimir touched my elbow.

"Your Highness will do us the honor of this dance." He said it like an order, not like a question.

I turned desperately to M. Creanga. "Is this compulsory?"

He looked stunned.

"I mean, it's just — you know, standing up for so long, and all these hoops. I might make a fool of myself." It sounded pretty lame, even to me.

"Your Highness does not wish to dance with us?" the prince demanded. His eyes grew narrow. He reminded me of someone. Someone. . . . I couldn't put my finger on it.

"Uh, no," I said, "it's nothing like that. I just —"

The look in his eyes convinced me that I definitely didn't want to dance with him, but the look on M. Creanga's face convinced me that I'd already committed a mammoth breach of etiquette.

"I only learned the waltz a few days ago," I explained. "And I just had a couple of lessons. I don't want you to be ashamed of me, that's all. Uh, do you think you could take off your sword while we're dancing?"

I pictured the silver blade slicing my ruffles to ribbons as we waltzed. That would probably be another breach of etiquette and I'd probably get blamed for it.

"We never take off our sword," the prince said. "Not while we are in uniform."

"Oh well. *C'est la vie,*" I sighed. "Let's boogie, Your Highness."

"We hope you do not dislike us," Casimir said, as we stumbled through the first waltz. "Perhaps we have just gotten off on the wrong foot. My little joke. Ho, ho."

"Truly amusing," I replied. "Don't say I didn't warn you about my dancing."

"You are enchanting. How could you imagine we would be ashamed of you? May we call you Dolores?"

"Oh, I wish you wouldn't. It's confusing enough around here without two Doloreses."

"But you are the only Dolores," he said. "Florinda the Fourteenth, heir to the throne of Saxony Coburn." He stared down at me, his eyes hot and piercing.

Up to now he had kept a respectable distance as we danced. The hoops in my skirt made sort of a protective cage around my body.

Maybe Mlle Chenille knew what she was doing after all.

"My beauty!" he murmured ardently. He grabbed me and clutched me against his chest.

"My skirt!" I shrieked.

The thing about a hoopskirt is that wherever the hoops go, the skirt goes, too. So when Casimir pulled me to him, his legs hit the metal hoops that made the dress stand out, and the back of the skirt shot straight up behind me, conking me on the back of the head.

"Let go of me!" I cried, trying to wrestle out of his grasp. "Don't you see what you're doing?"

There was sudden silence in the ballroom. Everybody was staring at us. *I'm going to die.* I am going to *die*. Is Geoffrey still here?

My mother, the princess, rushed toward us. I wrenched myself away from Casimir. Mummy yanked the back of my skirt down. The front of my skirt flew up and hit Casimir under the chin.

He looked horrified. He smacked at the hoop with both hands, pushing the skirt right back at Mummy.

The stunned silence was broken by an outburst of royal titters. My skirt swung back and forth before it finally settled down to a gentle sway. I was frozen to the floor.

Someone must have told Lester to hit it again, because the orchestra suddenly started to play.

"This is the most embarrassing thing that ever happened to me in my whole life," I moaned.

Geoffrey must be watching this whole farce. He must have seen my skirt shoot up. Sure, I was wearing about seventeen ruffled petticoats underneath it, but what a clod I must seem to him.

Mummy tried to repress a giggle. She failed. She patted her hair and dabbed at her flushed face with a lace handkerchief.

"Goodness, wasn't that an amusing little *contretemps*?"

"We are not amused!" I exclaimed. "We are covered with shame!"

She giggled again. "Fortunately, you were covered with petticoats, too, so no harm done."

This was the first hint I'd had that Mummy might have a sense of humor. Warped, perhaps, but a sense of humor.

"No good done, either," I said. "This doesn't exactly enhance my royal image. Everybody's been so concerned about me being proper and demure."

I turned to point an accusing finger at Casimir, to explain that the whole thing was his fault, but he had disappeared.

*Coward.*

"Now, now, my dearest, don't take yourself so seriously. My advice is to make a joke about this. You will put the others at their ease, and soon you will be laughing, too."

I couldn't believe it. Mummy has a conniption about my red mittens, she orders my clothes so drab that if I wore them near any woodwork, I'd fade right into it. But when one hundred and fifty of the self-crowned heads of Europe see my underwear, I mustn't take it seriously.

"Now come." She took my hand. "You will dance with the Count of Monte Cristo."

This was too much. "Wait a minute. You don't expect me to believe that? *The Count of Monte Cristo* is a book. He's a *fictional character*."

"Ah, no, *ma petite*. That was the other one."

# 12

All right, so there really is a Count of Monte Cristo. I danced with him. And then the King of Croatia, the Duke of Ürll, the Marquis de la Brioschi.

They all kept a safe distance from my hoopskirt.

The orchestra attempted some disco music, in my honor I assumed, and Papa asked me to dance with him to *Stayin' Alive*. He turned out to be a very good dancer, and I realized he must have requested the music himself.

Now that they were playing something at my speed, I was much more competent than I was at waltzing. And Papa was terrific. He bopped around, pointed his bejeweled finger at me once in a while, and singing, "Unhh, unhh, unhh, unhh," along with the music. The whole John Travolta bit.

The guests all stopped dancing to watch us. They hummed "Unhh, unhh, unhh, unhh," and tapped their feet to the beat.

When the song ended, everyone burst into applause. The prince leaned down to kiss my hand, and I curtseyed — which is one thing, at least, that you can do safely in a hoopskirt.

"You're a terrific dancer, Your Highness," I said.

"You're a pretty cool cat yourself. Call us Papa."

Prince Casimir reappeared.

"There goes the neighborhood," I muttered.

"We are deluged with self-hatred," he proclaimed, "to think we have caused our childhood sweetheart the least morsel of discomfort."

"It was a great, big chunk of discomfort," I retorted. "And I can't be your childhood sweetheart. I only met you an hour ago."

"But we have been engaged for nine years," he said reasonably, "so we are childhood sweethearts."

"You were engaged to *somebody* for nine years," I said, "but not to me."

"Children, children," Papa clucked. "The road of true love never does run smooth. Casimir, you must be understanding. After all, our daughter has only just met you."

And already hates you.

"There must be time to establish a meaningful relationship," he went on. "It cannot happen in one evening. And you, my little cabbage" — he patted my shoulder — "must give Prince Casimir a chance. A tiny mishap must not prejudice you against him."

But I had disliked Casimir before that "tiny mishap."

Maybe that meant Papa was right. Maybe I was prejudiced. I was prepared not to like him before I even laid eyes on him.

After all, I loved Geoffrey. And I didn't want to get married. Not before I was a veterinarian, anyway.

Where *was* Geoffrey? I looked quickly around the room. Had he left?

"Why don't you kids take a nice stroll on the balcony?" Papa suggested.

"All right," I agreed, "if you'll be our chaperone."

"It is A-OK for you to be alone with your betrothed," he replied. "You don't need a chaperone with Prince Casimir."

I don't need a chaperone with anyone *except* Casimir.

What have I gotten myself into?

"Go ahead," Papa urged. "Everything will be jim-dandy, you'll see."

*Don't bet the farm, Papa.*

He practically shoved us toward the French doors that opened onto the balcony.

There were several other couples taking in the air as we went outside. The balcony overlooked the formal gardens and the maze. There was a waist-high stone railing the length of the balcony, and potted trees were set here and there for decoration.

Casimir frowned. He grasped my hand. Hard.

"We must be alone," he said intensely. His eyes glittered in the moonlight.

"No, we mustn't." *Who did he look like?*

The population on the terrace was rapidly decreasing. One couple glanced our way and exchanged whispers, another couple smiled and winked at us, and all four guests walked back inside with exaggerated casualness.

In moments there was no one left outside except us, and one other man. He was leaning over the railing, way down at the opposite end of the balcony, looking out at the gardens.

"At last we are alone," the prince said.

"Almost. Except for that man over there."

But Casimir apparently didn't care about the man with his back to us. He kissed my hand, which he was still holding, then kissed my wrist and began to work his way up my arm to my shoulder.

"Your Highness, please!" I tried to pull my arm away.

He planted a fiery kiss on my shoulder and aimed for my lips. I twisted my head and his lips landed on my ear, which only seemed to inflame him more.

"Stop it!" I shrieked.

He let go of me suddenly, his eyes smoldering. "We are ablaze with passion for you," he hissed. "We cannot control our hot blood."

"You'd better control it, Prince," I said shakily. "You may not take liberties with my royal person."

"Of course we may," he said, matter-of-factly. He reached for me again. "You are our bride."

I jumped up from the bench and backed away from him.

*"Not yet, I'm not."* And I'd sooner die, I added silently.

He stood up, and for some reason I pictured a

snake uncoiling itself. I shuddered and took a few steps backward until I felt the bottom of my hoops bounce against the railing.

Casimir moved toward me, slowly, determinedly. His face was pale in the moonlight, but there was no mistaking the expression on it.

Tony Perkins! *That's* who he reminded me of. Tony Perkins in *Psycho.*

I didn't know whether to yell for help or to leap over the railing — or both. I trembled as he approached me. His eyes were almost hypnotic. I couldn't seem to move, couldn't think straight.

*Geoffrey*, I thought desperately. *Help!*

"Your Highnesses," someone said. "What a bit of luck."

I turned to see who it was, and gasped.

Geoffrey! He was the other man on the balcony! He stood between us, holding his camera.

My knees sagged. I felt the shock of disbelief — and love. Geoffrey had rescued me at exactly the moment I wished for him. I grabbed hold of the railing to keep from collapsing in a royal swoon.

Casimir snapped to attention and put his hand to his sword as if he were getting ready to turn Geoffrey into shish kebab.

"My readers would appreciate a picture of the royal couple in such a romantic setting," Geoffrey said. "If I may?"

"Of course you may," I said eagerly. I could almost see steam coming out of Casimir's ears. "Take as many pictures as you want. And listen, if you could get me some copies, I'd love to send them to America. Let's take a lot of different poses and then I can pick the ones I like best."

Oh, Geoffrey, I love you. . . .

" . . . on this joyous occasion, to drink a toast to our beloved daughter, Her Serene Highness, Princess Dolores Theodora Marie Celeste, Florinda the Fourteenth, and His Highness, Prince Casimir Clovis Fabian Alaric, who are to be joined in wedded bliss."

Everyone cheered and raised their champagne glasses.

Casimir and I stood up and acknowledged the congratulations with smiles and waves.

I think I smiled. I tried to.

But I didn't eat much of the elaborate supper that followed.

Because something was very strange about that wedding proclamation. It wasn't anything the princess said — it was something she *didn't* say.

There was no mention of a wedding date.

I had a terrible feeling of foreboding. Maybe they don't want me to know. Maybe they think that if I find out how soon I'm to be joined in wedded bliss — EEK! — I'll abdicate.

My hands shook as I reached for a water glass.

"Our shy little peach blossom," Prince Casimir murmured. "How it will thrill our senses to see you bloom with the joy of love."

I should have thrown myself off the balcony while the throwing was good.

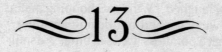

# 13

Prince Casimir stayed overnight at the palace after the ball to discuss "matters of state" with the prince and princess and M. Blitzen.

I guessed "matters of state" meant how much money he was going to sock into the treasury now that we were officially engaged.

Unfortunately, I was summoned to eat breakfast with them before the talks got underway.

"I have to call home — I mean, America, later," I said, even before I wished anyone a good morning. "I want to tell them the news."

"Certainly," Papa said.

I was kind of surprised he agreed so quickly.

"Maybe I'll go to town this morning and do some

shopping," I went on. *Anything* to get away from Casimir.

"The shops are closed on Sunday," Mummy said.

"Oh. Well, then I'll just window shop."

Casimir looked puzzled. "You have need of a window?"

Papa laughed. "Window shopping means looking in the windows and not buying anything."

"What a pointless waste of time." Casimir fingered his paisley silk ascot and brushed something invisible off the lapel of his white blazer.

"Really?" I said icily. "And how do you waste *your* time?"

He must have mistaken my tone of voice, because instead of looking insulted, his eyes lit up.

"You mean, what is our hobby? Taxidermy. We are a skilled taxidermist. You must see our collection."

*"You stuff dead animals?"* I cried.

"Of course. The live ones would never stand for it. Ho, ho."

The princess tittered politely at Casimir's attempt at humor, but Papa howled with delight.

"That is a good one, Casimir. The live ones wouldn't stand for it. Your fiancé is quite a wit, *ma petite*."

"He's a million laughs," I said. Casimir looked very pleased with himself.

"You will be astounded at some of our pieces," he went on. "We have several hummingbirds — very delicate work, hummingbirds. We even have a California condor."

I was appalled. "But that's an endangered species!"

"Not here," he said calmly.

Tony Perkins played a taxidermist in *Psycho*! Now the likeness was absolutely shuddermaking.

I couldn't believe it. This man they expected me to marry was going to lurk outside my operating room while I treated sick and wounded animals, and root for them to die so he could stuff them!

My first impression had been right.

Prince Casimir was a creep.

I'll call home the minute he leaves, I promised myself.

Jeannot walked to town with me while the prince and my royal parents talked money.

Dulsia was charming, but I was too distracted at the thought of my marriage to the taxidermist to fully appreciate what I was seeing.

Other people were about, taking advantage of the warm, clear day. They bowed and curtseyed and waved to me. I smiled and waved back.

The capital of Saxony Coburn was a storybook village. The streets were cobblestoned and many of the stores had candy-striped awnings. The only thing faintly modern about the town was the movie theater.

They were showing *The Wizard of Oz*.

We passed a bakery and flower shops and a shoemaker and some clothing stores. I glanced in the windows. The clothes weren't drop-dead chic, but most of them were more appealing than the maroon suit and white blouse I was wearing. Of course, a prison uniform would be more appealing than what I was wearing.

Suddenly I found myself in front of a large glass window with LA JOURNÉE stenciled on it in gold letters.

I finally perked up. "The newspaper office! Jeannot, let's go in and see if they developed the photos from the ball yet."

Geoffrey. Geoffrey is right behind these windows, right in back of this door. I reached for the brass handle.

"It is not available yet, Mademoiselle," Jeannot said.

I tried the door. It was locked.

"How can it be closed?" I demanded. "It's a *newspaper*. The news never stops."

"It will reopen itself this night," Jeannot said. "For the tomorrow *Journée*."

And Casimir will be gone by tonight.

As I let go of the doorknob, a cunning plan began to take shape in my mind.

My fiancé left, kissing my hand and both my cheeks. The prince and princess beamed with pleasure, and I shut my eyes tightly and prayed I wouldn't turn into a toad.

"I have to call America," I announced. "To tell them the . . . um . . . joyous news of my betrothal."

I was surprised again when the princess said, "Of course, my dear. Go right ahead. Use the phone in the morning room if you would like privacy."

I wondered why they weren't trying to discourage me from phoning home, as they usually did, but I was too relieved to look a gift horse in the mouth.

I definitely needed privacy.

Because I was going to make two calls. One was long distance. The other wasn't.

It took forever for the call to Kansas to go through. I held on, instead of having the operator ring me back when she reached my house. I wasn't going to take any chances on having this call intercepted.

Finally she announced she had my number.

The phone rang twice.

"Hello."

"Daddy! It's me. Your daughter, the princess. Listen, you've got to do something —"

" . . . nobody home except this machine you're talking to, so please leave your name and number. . . ."

I groaned. We never had a phone machine. My parents must have bought it after I left, to avoid all the curiosity-seekers and media people.

I waited for the sound of the beep, still hoping someone might answer the phone when they heard my voice.

*Beep.*

"Mom, Dad, it's me. If you're there, pick up the phone. If not, HELP! They're marrying me off to a taxidermist but I don't know when. Call me back as soon as you can, and make sure you speak to me *personally*."

Then I called Geoffrey.

Monday I started my normal schedule. Now that the ball was over, everyone promised me things would be less hectic.

My lessons were from nine-thirty to twelve-thirty. Dolores had always had them in the "schoolroom," but I asked Mme Banat if we could use the morning room. There was a phone in there.

Every time it rang I lunged for it. It rang a lot.

Mme Banat was getting more and more frustrated trying to teach me French between phone calls, but I had to be sure that no one was telling my parents that I was out.

"I'm expecting a call," I explained.

"You'll be notified if there is a call for you," she said.

"I'm not so sure about that," I muttered. "I get the feeling I'm not notified about anything around here."

"Why, Your Highness, what do you mean?"

"I mean, I have a lot of questions about a lot of things and nobody wants to answer me. Everyone's giving me the royal brush-off."

"You've been so busy. We've all been rushed. Ask me your questions. I won't give you the royal brush-off."

Why not? Mme Banat would know everything. After all, they had been planning the wedding while Dolores was still her pupil. And Dolores was so hot to marry Prince Casimir that she probably talked about it all the time.

"When am I supposed to marry this prince?" I asked.

Immediately Mme Banat's gray eyes shifted from my face. She looked past me. "The date is, as yet, undecided."

"See! You won't tell me, either. I don't believe

they haven't set the date for the wedding. The prince kept calling me his bride at the ball, and they were holed up talking money all day yesterday. I'll bet Casimir knows the date. He's paying for me. Don't tell me he doesn't care when I'm delivered!"

"But it's the truth, Your Highness. Originally Dolores was to be married on her sixteenth birthday. During the Gloxinia Festival."

"Sixteenth birth —" I tried to stand up. I had to grip the arms of the chair to steady myself. "You mean in three weeks? What about vet school? What about college? I'm only fifteen and eleven twelfths! And I'm very immature for my age!"

"Please try to be calm. If I may say so, you don't seem immature to me. And surely when you agreed to accept your crown, you didn't expect your life to go on exactly the way you planned it when you were an ordinary American citizen."

"That just goes to show you how immature I am," I said. "And when I agreed to be the princess, no one told me I had to get married in a month."

"You don't like Prince Casimir?" she asked.

"I don't want to get married to *anybody* in three weeks. I'm a kid. And I only met the guy Saturday night. I don't even know how old he is."

"The prince is twenty-four."

*And plays with dead birds.*

I'd suspected that the wedding would be fairly soon, but this was ridiculous.

I headed for the door. "So long," I said. "I'm abdicating."

"Mademoiselle, please listen before you abdicate. I said that was the *original* plan. Now your parents feel you need more time with them in the palace before you become a wife."

I stopped at the door. "Then it's not going to be in three weeks?"

"Things are done differently in America," Mme Banat went on. "Your parents understand that. And they feel you have a lot to learn about your royal obligations."

"That's right," I agreed eagerly. "My mother didn't raise me to be a princess." I began to see a glimmer of hope.

"I'm sure that much of yesterday's discussion had to do with postponing the marriage. No doubt Prince Casimir will resist a delay."

"No doubt," I repeated. "Resist" was putting it mildly. He'd probably throw himself on the floor and hold his breath until he turned blue.

"But how long will they postpone it?"

"That I don't know. But you won't be a June bride. Not *this* June." She smiled reassuringly.

I smiled back. What a relief. I was sure she was telling the truth. Her eyes were steady and sincere and she really seemed to care about my feelings.

"Okay," I said. "In that case, I won't abdicate."

After all, the wedding could be a year from now. Or two years. At least I didn't have to worry about being married off in twenty-one days. I'd have plenty of time to figure out a way to avoid marrying Casimir.

Of course, in the meantime I would have to figure out a way to avoid *Casimir*.

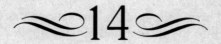

# 14

By Tuesday my parents still hadn't phoned, but I was so wrapped up in my secret plan to meet Geoffrey that I didn't spend much time worrying about them.

My trunk arrived that morning, which was a real break. Creating my disguise would be a lot easier now that I had my own clothes to use.

The minute I finished lunch I dashed to my chamber. It was one o'clock. I had half an hour to get ready.

I opened the trunk and dug frantically through the piles of clothes until I found what I was looking for.

*  *  *

When I called Geoffrey Sunday night, he sounded surprised to hear my voice. When I told him I had to see him, he sounded even more surprised.

But he recognized how upset I was and he must have been as anxious to see me as I was to see him, because he agreed immediately to a secret rendezvous.

And now, I thought, as I added one more coat of lipstick to the three I had already applied, now in just a few minutes we'll be together.

I stuck my head out the door of my room. This was the trickiest part of the whole plan. I had to get downstairs without being seen, and slip into the crowd of visitors touring the palace.

Once I started to mingle I was sure no one would recognize me, but if I was seen coming down the stairs, the whole plot would be discovered and I'd end up locked in my room until the wedding.

No one was in the hall, so I tiptoed to the head of the stairs. From there I could see the black and white tiled floor of the foyer and the oak doors of the entrance. Two uniformed guards stood at attention outside the open doors, with their backs to me.

I held my breath and waited for the first opportunity.

At any second, someone might emerge from one of the rooms behind me. A voice might call out, "What are you doing here?"

A few people trickled in: a mother with a little girl, two women in pants suits and plastic raincoats, an old man wearing a white fishing hat.

The public wasn't exactly beating down the doors to see the palace. Most of the Saxony Coburnians must have seen it already, and the tourist trade here was practically nonexistent, except maybe during the Gloxinia Festival.

I kept waiting for the right group.

Finally I heard a clamor of voices. A whole bunch of kids charged into the foyer, giggling and shouting, while two women tried to quiet them down. A class trip, I guessed.

This was it. Just the cover I needed. As the last few kids passed out of sight down the hall, I started down the stairs.

The guards still had their backs to the doors. I couldn't see any tourists outside. Praying that none of the maids or Mlle Grusk would suddenly pop into the foyer, I sped silently down the stairs and shot straight through the hallway.

I followed the sound of the children's voices to the portrait gallery.

They swarmed around the room, making a lot of noise while their teachers tried to point out the historical portraits that lined the walls.

The kids were kind of cute. I probably thought they were even more adorable than they really were, since they made such a commotion that no one paid the slightest attention to me as I slipped into the gallery.

The old man with the hat was studying a portrait of Florinda I. Three portraits away from him, a gorgeous blond man in jeans and leather jacket was checking his watch.

*Geoffrey.* I wanted to run right through the herd

109

of children, scattering them like chickens, and throw my arms around him. But I didn't.

I took a long, deep breath and walked slowly along the edge of the room till I reached him.

"Geoffrey." I touched his arm gently.

He nearly jumped. "Your High —" He stopped himself, flustered. "Is that you?"

"Nifty disguise, isn't it?" I whispered.

He looked from the blue scarf I'd tied around my forehead like a headband, to the dark sunglasses, the dark red lipstick, the extremely oversized sweater, right down to the skirt that came to my ankles. I hadn't had a chance to hem it after I bought it, which just goes to show you that procrastination sometimes pays off.

"You don't look very inconspicuous," he whispered.

"Yeah, but I don't look like you-know-who, either."

"I like the way you-know-who looks," he said quietly. "If I may say so."

"You certainly may," I replied. You may say much more, too, if you like.

"Geoffrey, we're breaking out of this joint and you're my ticket to freedom."

He grinned. "That sounds like a James Cagney prison movie."

"Could be. I know just how he felt. Now, here's my plan. The last room on the tour is the ballroom. We shoot straight over there, mingle with a group that's leaving, and just walk right out the front doors."

"Your High —"

*"Shh!"*

*"Abby —"*

"Shh!"

"Mademoiselle," he said desperately.

I nodded.

"You didn't tell me about this part of the plan. I can't sneak you out of the palace and take you off without a chaperone. We'd be in really big trouble if we were caught."

I was flabbergasted. "You mean you don't want to be alone with me? I thought —" I stopped myself.

Didn't he like me? Or didn't he like me enough to take a chance on getting in big trouble? My heart sank.

"We'd better start walking," he said. "We're supposed to be looking at the paintings."

I followed him silently, miserably, as he began to move around the gallery. He spoke to me in French and gestured at a portrait once in a while. A few more people entered the room. The children left.

He sat down on an iron bench in front of an etching of the palace. He motioned for me to sit next to him.

"I want to be alone with you very much," he said softly.

"But not enough to take a teensy little chance of getting caught." I thought I might cry.

Geoffrey, my hero and protector. Geoffrey, who rescued me from Casimir with his flash camera and press pass, was a coward at heart.

"I have a loyalty to my country and to the royal

family," he said. "I don't want to stir up another scandal, and I don't want you to be disgraced and vilified."

"I don't know what you're talking about," I said, "but I'm part of the royal family, remember? I mean, I don't want to pull rank on you, but . . . I thought you — I mean, I wish you wanted — oh, just forget the whole thing."

It was lucky I was wearing my dark glasses, because now I did start to cry.

Geoffrey didn't love me at all. I don't know how I could have mistaken that electricity I felt the first time we met, but I must have.

And if Geoffrey wouldn't help me, if he didn't feel the same powerful attraction to me that I felt toward him — then I was completely alone.

A tear slid down past my sunglasses. I closed my eyes tightly, trying to stop it, but a whole lot of others followed it down my cheeks.

"Your Highness, please don't cry," he pleaded. I was so upset that I didn't even remind him not to call me Your Highness. Anyway, what use was my disguise now that my whole scheme was blown out of the water?

I could order him to carry on with the escape plan, but I couldn't order him to love me. Kiss me, maybe, but who wants to be kissed by someone who has to be commanded to kiss you?

"Your Highness," he whispered, "you must know that there are so many things I want to say to you that I can't say. When I saw you at the ball with the prince, I felt — I can't even begin to describe how I felt."

"Try," I sniffled.

Geoffrey hesitated a moment. "I wanted to beat him senseless and carry you off on my moped."

"Oh, *Geoffrey*!" I started to cry even harder. He did love me! He did want to rescue me from Casimir the Creep.

He pulled out a handkerchief. He looked around the room. We were alone.

"May I touch you?" he asked.

"Touch me, touch me," I nodded.

He dabbed at my cheeks with the handkerchief. He took my hand and helped me up. He led me to a corner of the gallery where we could see people come in before they saw us.

He put his hands on my shoulders and looked down at me. His eyes were grave and troubled.

"May I —" He seemed to be struggling with his emotions — or against them.

"Oh, I wish you would," I sighed.

He slipped my sunglasses off and looked deep into my eyes. He bent his head and kissed me softly and carefully on the lips. He touched my cheek, my hair, ran his finger over my eyebrow. I couldn't breathe, I couldn't move.

"Geoffrey," I whispered.

"Your Highness," he said urgently. And before I could tell him not to call me Your Highness, his arms were around me and his mouth was on mine and there was nothing cautious about his kiss this time.

"I'm sorry," he said. "I'm sorry, Your Highness, I —"

"What for?" I asked weakly. "You did fine."

He seemed to be having trouble catching his breath. I know I was.

"I did a terrible thing," he groaned.

"But you did it so *well*."

Suddenly I heard voices outside the gallery.

I grabbed his handkerchief. "Quick! You're wearing more lipstick than I am." I wiped his lips and shoved the handkerchief back into his jacket pocket. I put my sunglasses on.

A young couple walked into the gallery holding hands. I pulled Geoffrey toward the door. Three more people came in and I could hear the sound of the children not far off.

"Let's go," I said. "Look nonchalant. Speak French."

We walked out of the portrait gallery. The schoolchildren were just coming out of the ballroom. They passed us and I tugged Geoffrey's hand, turned around, and followed them.

"Where are we going?" Geoffrey asked.

"Out."

"But I told you —"

"I decided to pull rank after all. Just stick with the kids and act casual. I have it all figured out."

"You don't," he protested. "You don't have anything figured out. There are things you don't know — "

"That's one of the reasons we have to get out of here. So you can tell me all the things I should have been told before I got here."

And after Geoffrey answered my questions, we ought to have a good half hour left before I had to get back to the palace.

If things went the way I hoped, it would be a *very* good half hour.

*"Come on,"* I said. "The kids are making such a racket nobody will notice us."

The children burst out of the palace like they'd just been released from school for the summer. We slipped out after them, into the blazing sunlight.

"We did it!" I crowed. "See, no problem. Now all we have to do is —"

The man counting the money in the collection box looked up, startled, as we passed.

"Mr. Torunga! You were not expected today. What are you doing here?"

It was M. Blitzen.

"Your Highness!" he cried. "What are *you* doing?"

"Uh —" Think fast, Your Highness. "Working on my tan?"

# ~15~

The War Room was furnished with a long, dark wood table and high-backed chairs. A huge globe on a stand took up one corner of the room. In front of a narrow window stood a desk with two telephones, an inkstand, and a quill pen.

"We call this the War Room," Prince Albert said, "although we haven't had any wars in four hundred years."

"Why break a four-hundred-year-old tradition?" I asked nervously. I wondered how far the dungeon was from here.

The prince and princess sat at one end of the table, with M. Creanga and M. Blitzen on either side of them. I sat way down at the other end of the table, feeling very small and very intimidated.

And I didn't know why! What had I done that was so terrible?

"Do I have a right to get a lawyer?"

"This is not a trial," the princess said.

"You could have fooled me. Listen, why is everyone so upset? All I wanted was a little walk. I'm getting claustrophobia in this place."

"Your phobia may get worse before it gets better," M. Blitzen warned. "Your actions threatened the fate of our entire country."

"Oh, come now. What's so awful about what I did? Couldn't you look at it as sort of a childish prank? How could an innocent little stroll through the gardens threaten the whole country?"

"I think," the prince said, "we must lay our cards on the table and be out front about the matter."

"Good thinking," I agreed. "It's about time someone told me what's going on around here." I remembered what Geoffrey had said about causing a scandal. Dolores said I'd already caused a scandal. And M. Creanga had mentioned it, too.

What scandal could I possibly have caused? I didn't even get to Saxony Coburn until last Sunday.

"Dolores," the princess began.

"Call me Abby."

"*Dolores,*" she repeated firmly. "We will call you Dolores because that is who you are and you must always remember that. You have been told that you may not be unchaperoned with any man except Prince Casimir. You are not permitted to fall in love with a commoner."

"Fall in love? Me, in *love*? Ha ha."

Boy, did that sound weak.

"By the way — not that I care or anything — but what are you going to do to Geoffrey?"

"You will forget about Mr. Torunga," M. Blitzen said. "You will not see him again."

"What did you do to him?" I cried.

"We have been making allowances for you," the princess went on. "We know that this is a difficult adjustment. We have been trying to persuade Casimir to be patient while you become accustomed to life here, and your duties to the crown."

"I appreciate that," I said, "but —"

"However, perhaps it is a mistake to postpone your wedding. The safest thing to do now seems to be to get you satisfactorily wed, before you give Prince Casimir cause to call off the nuptials."

*"What?"*

The prince tried to smile.

"I don't like Casimir! Casimir is creepy! I'm fifteen years old! I want my mother!"

"We are your mother," the princess reminded me.

"No, you're not. If you were, you'd care about how I feel."

"We do care," the prince said, distressed.

"But we cannot take feelings into consideration," M. Creanga said. "This marriage has nothing to do with feelings."

"I know, I know!" I yelled. "It's all money. Casimir's money. Well, let me tell you something. He'll never call off the wedding, if that's what you're

118

worried about. I make his blood hot and his passions blaze. Blecchh," I added.

"Meaning no offense, Your Highness," M. Creanga cut in, "but the prince's blood boils very easily."

"As does yours, Mademoiselle," remarked M. Blitzen. "If I may say so."

"You may not!" I said. "You can't talk to me that way. Can he?" I asked the prince.

The princess sighed. She pulled out a folded piece of paper and handed it to the prince.

"Must we?" the prince said.

"We must," she replied.

He handed the paper to M. Creanga. "Pass it down."

M. Creanga got up and brought the paper to me.

"What's this?" I unfolded it and saw that it was palace stationery with my handwriting on it.

*Dear Carol,*

*. . . I'm in love with a commoner. He's the reporter who came to interview me. . . .*

"Where did you get this?" I demanded. "Now you've got people spying on me?"

"We have no spies," the princess said. "Dolores found it in your room and brought it to us."

Dolores. That sneak. That tattletale. That fink. *I'll get her*, I vowed. *And her little dog, too.*

"What right does she have to go pawing through my things?"

"She has no right," the princess said. "But she did, and she found this. We must do something about it before you and Mr. Torunga cause another scandal."

"What *is* all this stuff about a scandal?" I looked from face to face, waiting for an explanation. No one said anything.

The prince cleared his throat. "Let us take it from the top," he began. "When Dr. Zdenka died, he left a letter describing the circumstances of your birth."

I nodded. I knew this part. "He was drunk and mixed the babies up."

"That meant that Dolores was not a legitimate heir to the throne. She was, in fact, a commoner. Of course, no way would Prince Casimir wed a commoner."

"Perish the thought," I said.

The prince nodded. "Our economy has been depressed for years. The only thing that gave our people hope was knowing that they just had to hang in there until Casimir married Dolores and infused our treasury with his funds."

"A knight in shining money," I muttered.

"But Dolores did not object," the princess said. "She wanted to marry Casimir. It broke her poor heart to find out she could not." She touched a lace handkerchief to her eyes.

"Why did anyone have to know?" I asked. "You could have hushed up the whole thing, couldn't you?"

"It crossed our mind," the prince admitted, "but we could not bring ourselves to corrupt the royal lineage."

"And the letter was given to Samson Torunga," the princess added.

"Geoffrey's father," I said softly. "The editor of the newspaper. Now I get it."

"When the news came out," M. Creanga went on, "the people were incensed. There was animosity against the royal family. Dolores was the particular target of the citizens' outrage."

"That's why she stays inside all the time," I said.

The princess was in tears. Suddenly I began to feel sorry for them all — even Dolores.

"We announced that you were coming to Saxony Coburn before we even knew if we could find you," the prince said. "And finding you was no piece of cake, my dear."

"But the people were not appeased," said M. Creanga. "There was great unrest. There were even demonstrations. Two hundred plastic raincoats were burned in the palace courtyard."

"The odor was dreadful," the princess sniffed.

"The greenhouse workers refused to water the gloxinias. The Gloxinia Festival was threatened. Some of our young people marched in front of the palace, chanting, 'Yankee go home.'"

"That is why it was so vital to bring you here immediately," M. Blitzen explained. "And that is why we cannot allow you to do anything that would jeopardize your marriage to Prince Casimir."

"Which you conveniently forgot to tell me about before I got here," I pointed out.

Nobody would meet my eye.

"Therefore, until the day of the wedding," M. Blitzen said, "you will not leave the palace without a chaperone, and Mr. Torunga will not be permitted entry to the palace at all. The switchboard operator will obtain permission from the prince or princess before she places any calls for you."

"You mean, I can't even talk to my parents? *You can't do this to me!* You can't keep me a prisoner for two years!"

"It will not be for two years," the prince said hastily. "We would not do that to our daughter. As we told you, the wedding will not be postponed."

"You mean —"

"You will only be confined for three weeks."

*"Three weeks!* You're going back to the original plans? *I'm going to marry that taxidermist in less than a month?"*

"On your birthday," the princess said happily. "During the Gloxinia Festival."

I sprang out of my chair and made a mad dash for the door. "I won't do it! You can't make me! I resign. I'm abdicating. *I want to go home.*"

"But you *are* home, my dear," the prince said gently.

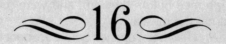

# 16

**KANSAS TEEN BECOMES PRINCESS; HIGH SCHOOL GIRL
TO RULE SAXONY COBURN**

(Kansas City Star, page 1)

**KANSAS KUTIE KOPS KROWN—NETWORK
NABOBS VIE FOR MOVIE RIGHTS**

(Variety, page 1)

**AMERICAN GIRL DISCOVERED TO BE PRINCESS
IN SHOCKING BIRTH-SWITCH SCANDAL!!!**

(National Enquirer, page 1)

*U.S. Student to Assume Crown*
(The New York Times, page 26)

My parents sent the articles, along with a letter that said they were going camping for two weeks in the Rockies, and then on to Hollywood to discuss movie deals.

No wonder they'd never returned my call. And no wonder the prince and princess hadn't tried to stop me from calling them. My parents wrote that they'd phoned before they left, and were promised that I'd get the message.

The letter had been opened before Jeannot brought it to me. All my letters were opened before I saw them. There might even have been mail I never saw.

I don't know if I was angrier at the thought of my folks going merrily off on vacation without spending part of it visiting me, or because I now had two sets of parents raking in megabucks from my plight.

"I'm truly all alone, Toto," I sighed. I reached down and patted the dog's head. I didn't have to reach down much. Toto was a Great Pyrenees, and enormous.

The prince gave him to me the day after the meeting in the War Room.

"We thought he would be good company for you," he said kindly. "He is very well-trained."

The dog leaned his head against my hip and licked my hand as we were introduced. He nearly pushed me over. He must have weighed a hundred pounds, and if he stood on his hind legs, he could easily rest his head on top of mine.

No matter how sulky and uncooperative I felt, I couldn't resist him.

"We hope you like him," the prince said. "He

certainly seems to cotton to you."

"I like him very much," I said coolly. "He's the Shetland pony I never had. Come, Toto."

"He only speaks French," the prince said. "His name is *Pierre de bonne chance*."

But Toto was already following me up the stairs. Except to be walked and fed, he hadn't left my side since.

And I hadn't left my room since.

For three days now I'd refused to come out. I wouldn't take my lessons, wouldn't eat my meals with the prince and princess, and refused to go to the photographer's to have my picture taken for my postage stamp.

I wouldn't speak to anyone except Jeannot and Toto.

I put aside the letter from my parents and shoved the clippings into my desk drawer.

"You know something?" I said to Toto. He cocked his head to one side and listened attentively. "It seems to me that this sulking is getting us absolutely nowhere. As long as I keep myself locked up, I'm just making it easier for everyone. Nobody has to worry about me causing any trouble, or —"

I stopped myself. Of course! That's it!

"What a dope I am," I groaned.

I started pacing the room. Toto got up and paced with me.

"I tried to be a good princess. Until they pulled this marriage bit — I mean, I was ready to take a shot at ruling Saxony Coburn. I cooperated and I did everything I was told, and they all thought I was a peachy princess."

I walked over to the closet and pulled out a short red skirt and my roller skates.

"So what did that get me?" I pulled off my jeans and put on the skirt. "Betrothed, that's what it got me."

I sat down on the rug and pulled on my roller skates. I laced them up and Toto chewed on the laces.

I clumped across the rug toward the door. Toto looked doubtfully at my skates.

"Therefore and ergo," I said, "the way to get unbetrothed and deprincessed is to be a perfectly putrid princess. Which I cannot be if I stay in this room watching Bulgarian television."

I picked up my stereo and Toto's leash.

"Come on, Toto. You can help me. We're going to turn ourselves into a royal pain."

The dog got up eagerly and trotted toward me. I pulled open my chamber door, and started to hum *The Skater's Waltz* as I glided down the hall to the stairs.

"Neat skating rink, *n'est-ce pas*, Toto?" I had to shout to be heard over the Def Leppard cassette. Fifteen minutes of running alongside me as I zoomed around the grand ballroom had gotten Toto used to the skates — though I wasn't sure he'd ever get used to Def Leppard.

I felt great. The exercise was doing me a lot of good. The loud music raised my spirits; this was the first time since I'd been in Saxony Coburn that I was doing something *I* wanted to do.

Except for kissing Geoffrey, of course. But I'd

manage that, too, before this campaign was over.

"Okay, Toto, now we're going to try something a little different." I clipped his leash to his collar and held onto the end with both hands. "Start running," I said. "Um, *marchez vite!*"

Toto was probably a little overexcited by this time, and very enthusiastic about our workout.

I started to skate and Toto started to run. In an instant he was running ahead of me, pulling me along after him like a water-skier.

"Whee!" I shouted. "Good dog! Smart dog! *Strong* dog!"

We zipped down to the end of the ballroom where the band had played during the ball, and Toto hung a screaming left at the bandstand.

"Watch that cornering!" I fought to keep my balance as he wheeled around to race back.

"Slow down!" I whipped sideways. I balanced on one skate, struggling to bring my left foot down before my right foot shot forward and I landed on my backside.

"Centrifugal force, Toto!" I barely managed to get my left foot down as Toto zoomed back the length of the ballroom. "Remember, centrifugal force!"

If "slow down" was not in Toto's vocabulary, he probably didn't know Thing One about centrifugal force, but he was a very intelligent dog, and I *had* spent two days teaching him English commands.

Now, I am not a world class skater, and Toto was brand-new at this and, as we flew toward the other end of the ballroom, I began to realize that I might not be in complete control of the situation.

At which moment the princess and Mlle Grusk

rushed into the ballroom, stopped stock still just inside the door, and stared, open-mouthed, as we hurtled toward them.

"Sit, Toto!" I cried desperately. *"S'assieds* yourself!"

Obediently, Toto slid to a screeching halt and sat.

I felt the leash rip out of my hand as I shot forward, past Toto.

There was no way to stop myself.

"Look out!" I yelled.

The two women leaped in opposite directions. I flew right between them, out the doors, into the hallway, and smack into a suit of armor.

"Did you hurt yourself, my dear?" the princess asked. She and Mlle Grusk watched anxiously as I staggered away from the armor.

"I can't say I did myself any good."

"As long as you are not injured," the princess said cheerily. "We are so glad to see you finally enjoying yourself."

I just gaped at her for a minute. This wasn't the reaction I'd expected at all.

"I guess you don't want me to skate in here," I said. "I mean, the floor is probably going to get ruined from my skates."

"Not at all. Your wheels are plastic. The floor is marble. It is an ideal place to skate. You must be careful, though. It is not an ideal place to fall."

I was getting a little frustrated. Why didn't she criticize me for actions unbecoming a princess?

"I suppose my skirt is shamefully short," I hinted.

"It is a skating skirt. It is suitable for the activity. We think you look quite *sportive*."

This was driving me nuts. Why was she being so agreeable? Why wasn't she reading me the royal riot act?

"The music," I said, in a last-ditch attempt. "I have to play the music loud, you know. It's the only way to listen to it."

"Yes." The princess nodded thoughtfully. "The music is not exactly our cup of tea."

Aha! Now I knew how to get to her. Loud rock, night and day — I'd drive everyone berserk. (Except maybe the prince.)

"But we can close these doors," she said, "whenever you wish to skate, and no one will even hear the music."

*I give up.* Round One goes to Princess Florinda XIII.

I stroked across the room to get my stereo.

"Are you finished skating?" the princess asked.

Skating, yes. Finished, no.

*I have just begun to be a royal pain.*

I agreed to go to the photography studio to pose for my stamp. The princess was delighted. I dressed for my portrait in a Mickey Mouse sweat shirt and jeans.

Mlle Grusk seemed a little startled as we got into the black Mercedes, but the princess didn't seem the least bit perturbed.

"This is one of my favorite shirts," I announced, as the car purred up the cobblestone street to the photographer's shop. "I wear it all the time. It probably won't look too dignified on a stamp, though."

"Do not worry about your Mickey Mouse outfit," the princess said. "M. Mèlies will take only head shots. You will be draped with a white sheet."

I gnashed my teeth in frustration.

Round Two, to Florinda the XIII.

Obviously, more drastic action was necessary.

*I would rather die than marry Casimir. I am going to hang myself from the nearest gargoyle. Good-bye, cruel world.*

I slipped the note under the door to the royal chamber. I bundled up my bed sheet and climbed two flights of stairs to the top floor of the palace. Toto trailed at my side, making pounces at a corner of the sheet as it dragged on the floor.

I checked my palace map to find the Gothic wing. The rooms up here were mostly used for storage. Everything was dim and musty, even though the sun shone brightly outside.

"Aha. Here we are. There ought to be a gargoyle right outside this window."

The room was crammed with dusty cartons and wooden crates. Toto sneezed.

"Don't worry, Toto. I'm not really going to kill myself. I'm just going to scare them."

I looked out the window that faced the square in front of the palace. Sure enough, right underneath the window, a gargoyle projected from the stone wall. The window opened with a crank, but the crank wouldn't turn. It was frozen stuck.

"Great," I muttered, "just great. A person can't even stage a fake suicide in this place without running into problems."

I pushed and pulled at the crank, but it didn't budge.

"Come on, Toto," I sighed. "We have to go find another gargoyle."

I got lucky on the third window I tried. The crank turned easily when I tested it. Toto thought this was a neat game. He danced around as I opened the leaded glass window all the way. He barked happily and tried to kill the bed sheet.

"Now all I have to do is climb out there, sit on the gargoyle, and wait for them to come talk me out of it. I'll tie one end of the sheet to the gargoyle, and one end —"

Toto grabbed a piece of the sheet in his teeth and pulled.

"Toto, stop it!" I pulled back. Toto's tail wagged like mad.

"Let go of the sheet!" I yelled. "I don't want to play tug of war now! I've got to get out on that gargoyle before — oh, I give up. Keep the sheet."

I dropped my end. "I can do it without the sheet."

I leaned out the window. I looked down four stories to the ground. All I had to do was sit on the window ledge and slide down onto the gargoyle. It was right beneath me.

I could straddle it like a horse. I could hold onto its head. I could slip off and plunge four stories to my death.

I gulped. Maybe I could just sit on the window ledge. I'd put one leg over it, and when the prince and princess came running in to stop me they would think they'd gotten there just in time.

I put my foot on the ledge.

Toto growled.

"What's the matter? Look, I'll play sheet with you later. Now I've got to do this."

Toto growled again. He jumped at the window, put his paws on the sill, and grabbed hold of my pants leg with his teeth.

"Toto, I just want to put my leg out the window. It's not really —"

He pulled at my pants leg and whined.

"Listen, this is very heroic of you, but I don't need to be rescued. I'm just —"

Toto placed both paws over my leg and then put his great big head on top of his paws.

"Toto, get *off* me. This is very uncomfortable. Sit! *S'assieds*, will you?"

Toto didn't *s'assieds*.

"I never should have let you watch that Lassie movie."

I heard feet pounding in the hallway, and shrieks, and people yelling in French. The princess burst into the room, panting. "Dolores, Dolores, don't do it! We will talk. We will try to understand."

At last I had gotten a rise out of her. At last they would take my refusal to marry Casimir seriously. Now they'd see they couldn't keep me here against my will.

"Come away from the window," the prince pleaded.

By this time, my leg was getting stiff, and my other leg, the one I was standing on, was getting wobbly around the ankle.

But, I realized, I had them right where I wanted them. (The prince and princess, not my legs.) I was in a perfect position — so to speak — to make a few demands.

"I want to see Geoffrey," I said.

"We will arrange it," the princess said. "Do not jump."

"I want the wedding postponed until I can talk to my parents in America."

"We will arrange it," the prince said. "Please come away from the window."

Actually, I couldn't have pulled my leg back inside if I had wanted to. Toto still had it pinned to the sill.

"I want to call my friend Carol in America," I said. "And my friend Josh. And anyone else I feel like calling. I have no one to talk to here. I'm lonely."

"You may make phone calls," the princess said.

"We will spend more time with you," the prince said. "We will play Trivial Pursuit."

My mind raced, trying to think of anything more I might wangle out of them while the wangling was good.

"I want to be able to walk around outside by myself — without a chaperone."

"We will call off your guards," the prince promised.

"You've got a deal." I patted Toto's head. "Okay, hero. You can stop rescuing me now. Everything's going to be all right."

# 17

"Geoffrey!" My heart leaped as M. Creanga ushered him into the morning room.

"I am honored that you asked to see me, Your Highness. I was under the impression that I was *persona non grata* around here."

Oh, rats, he was going all formal again. Well, that was probably because of M. Creanga.

"Not anymore. We can see each other as much as we want."

I held out my hand. Geoffrey hesitated a moment, then bent his head and kissed me lightly on the knuckles.

*Look out, lips, it's your turn next.*

"You may go now, M. Creanga," I said haughtily.

"No, I may not." He settled into a chair in front of the fireplace and opened a leather portfolio on his lap.

"Listen, I don't want to be rude, but don't get comfortable. I want you to leave."

"Believe me, I am not comfortable. But I cannot leave."

"Why not?" I demanded. "The princess promised I could see Geoffrey."

"You *are* seeing him. You were not promised that you could see him alone."

Geoffrey was beginning to look confused.

"But that was *implicit*!" I protested.

I racked my brain trying to think up the exact wording of the promise the princess had made.

"Okay," I said abruptly, "we'll take a walk outside. I'm allowed to go out by myself without anyone following me around."

M. Creanga stood up and closed his portfolio.

"*Now* what are you doing?" I asked. "I made it very clear that I wanted to go outside by myself without — oh, no!"

M. Creanga nodded. "*By yourself*," he said. "Not with anyone else."

"I do not wish to cause you any trouble, Your Highness," Geoffrey said. He started for the door.

"I've been hoodwinked!" I cried. "This is a gyp!"

I threw myself down on the sofa. I'd counted on being alone with Geoffrey long enough to plot my escape route from Saxony Coburn. Once we devised a plan to get me out of here before the Gloxinia Festival, I thought we could get down to serious

135

business, like kissing, hugging, and swearing eternal devotion to one another.

I sighed and patted the cushion next to me. "Come on, Geoffrey. Don't go yet. At least we can talk."

He perched himself on the edge of the sofa, as if he wanted to be ready to make a quick exit.

"So," I began, "read any good books lately?"

"Abby!" Carol shrieked. "Is it really you? Why didn't you write? I called your folks to find out how you were, but they weren't home."

"They went to Hollywood to cash in on my fame," I said sourly. "I think I'm going to be a mini-series."

"That's incredible! Listen, can you hear me? This isn't a very good connection."

"We're probably being bugged," I said.

"What? Why should we be bugged? Abby, is everything all right? What's happening over there?"

I shouted to be heard over the static.

"THEY'RE HOLDING ME PRISONER! THEY'RE —"

The line went dead. No Carol, no static, no nothing.

"Carol? *Carol!*"

I jiggled the buttons on the receiver. Nothing.

I slammed the receiver back on the hook and hurled the phone at the fireplace.

"This is an outrage!" I howled as I stormed upstairs.

I burst into the royal bedchamber. "You lied! You all lied to me!"

The room was empty.

I grabbed the princess's phone and dialed the

palace operator. "You cut me off in the middle of my call! Get me that number again."

"*Je regrette*, Mademoiselle. The telephone has broken itself."

"Oh, yeah? I can imagine how it broke itself. You hear me, don't you? There's nothing wrong with this phone."

"Inside the palace, *oui*. Outside, *non*."

"How convenient!"

I was seething as I stomped down the hall to my own chamber.

These were very tricky people I was dealing with. I should have known better than to trust their promises. They would have promised me anything to keep me from throwing myself out the window.

Why hadn't I realized that before?

I was as much a prisoner as I was before my fake suicide.

And I'll bet, I thought grimly, they're not even going to play Trivial Pursuit with me.


"Prince Casimir!" Jeannot announced excitedly. "He is here. He desires to see you."

"He can desire anything he wants," I grumbled. "*Je reste ici.*"

"Do you wish me to deliver him to here?" she asked. "To your chamber?"

"*God*, no! Just tell him to go away."

"Go away? Your prince? You pull my foot, Your Highness."

"I'm not pulling your foot!" I snapped. "I don't want —"

Wait a minute. Refusing to see Casimir would

just make him crazier to see me than ever. What happened to my plan to be a putrid princess?

All right. So I suffered a little setback. But I couldn't just give up, and I couldn't sit around hoping to be miraculously rescued. I was the only person who could save me now.

What if Casimir found out what a royal pain I was? What if he discovered how obnoxious I could be when I really put my mind to it? If *Casimir* called off the wedding. . . .

Saxony Coburn might go bankrupt, but what choice did I have? If M. Creanga and M. Blitzen had leveled with me at the beginning, we wouldn't be in this predicament.

As far as I was concerned, it was now every princess for herself.

"I'll see him, Jeannot," I declared. "Just help me get dressed."

Jeannot looked very distressed as Toto and I went to meet Casimir. She begged me to say that she had been knocked unconscious by thugs, and I'd had to dress without her.

I was wearing my Mickey Mouse sweat shirt and the long skirt I'd worn to meet Geoffrey in the portrait gallery. It came right to the tips of my hiking boots.

I'd used almost an entire can of mousse fixing my hair so it stood out from the top and sides of my head in big spikes. Huge neon hoop earrings, which Carol had urged me to buy because *she* wanted them, completed my outfit.

The effect was dazzling. I looked like a punk peasant.

Casimir stared as I clumped downstairs toward him, Toto at my heels.

"Your Highness? My divine Dolores? Can this be you?"

"I don't know. I'll check." I looked down into my shirt and felt my arms. "Yup, it's me. Why are you staring like that? Don't you like the way I look?"

"Oh, yes, yes." He backed away. "I was merely admiring of your shirt. Mickey Mouse. Very droll."

"No, I think it's cotton jersey. You like my new hairstyle? I'm going to wear it this way for the wedding. Mlle Chenille is designing a special veil that we'll attach with a big gold safety pin."

Even mentioning the word wedding gave me chills. Any day now Mlle Chenille would be starting to make my bridal gown.

I shuddered. *Obnoxious*, I reminded myself. Obnoxious is my byword.

Before this day is over, Prince Casimir has to run, screaming, from the palace.

The prince didn't say a word. He was still staring.

"Well, enough of this chitchat," I said. "How about a stroll in the gardens? The calla lilies are in bloom again."

"It is my most extreme wish to have another romantic interlude with you," said Casimir.

"Then this is your lucky day, Toots."

Or mine.

The two guards at the palace entrance did a double take as I emerged. They were obviously not familiar with the punk peasant look.

"How come you're saying 'I' and 'me' instead of 'we' and 'us' today? You're not using the royal 'we' anymore?" I asked curiously.

"Now that we are on such intimate terms," Casimir oozed, "I believe we will dispose with the formalities."

"You better not dispose with all of them, buster."

We started walking toward the maze. Toto wagged his tail and wedged himself between us. Casimir looked down at the dog and frowned. He moved to the right side. Toto hung back for a second, then pushed himself in between us again.

I giggled. "Good dog."

"Perhaps the animal does not accompany us?" Casimir said, annoyed.

"Killer never leaves my side," I said firmly.

Casimir moved back to my left and took my arm. Toto frisked around us, circled us twice, and scampered in between our legs, playfully butting the prince in the hip.

"Neat game, eh, Killer?"

"Killer" was getting a little carried away. Just as we reached the entrance to the maze he suddenly dashed off, running at full stride in the direction of the garages.

"Come back, Killer!" I called. *"Venez!"*

Casimir smiled with satisfaction. "Let him have his romp," he said. He grabbed my elbow. "We will romp in the maze."

Before I could say, "No way, José," Casimir dragged me halfway down the first path of the maze.

The maze was a complicated series of twists and

turns, with seven-foot-high hedges bordering the walkways. There was only one path into the center and one path out. Once you made the first turn, and couldn't see the entrance anymore, you could get hopelessly lost trying to get anywhere.

A map of the maze was provided for palace visitors, but I'd never studied it. I just glanced at it long enough to see that the maze was full of wrong turns and dead ends.

Once Casimir got me inside, I'd never find my way out.

"Let go of me, you brute!" I tried to wrench free but I couldn't break his grip on my arm. We were headed for the first turn.

"Toto!" I yelled.

"Toto?" The prince stopped just at the end of the path. His fingers loosened for a moment. "Is that a game?"

I yanked my arm free and tried to run past him. He jumped sideways and blocked my way. I darted to the other side and he darted to the other side. I shifted to the right and the prince shifted along with me.

I couldn't get past him. He hounded me like a basketball guard, blocking every maneuver I tried.

*"Toto!"* I screamed.

"This is a good game," the prince said delightedly. "I see I must catch you."

I saw he mustn't catch me. I also saw I was never going to get past him and out of the maze. So even though I knew it was crazy, I turned into the maze, cutting left at the first intersecting path.

I'd never find my way out, and Toto would

probably never be able to find his way in to save me, even if he heard me, but maybe the prince wouldn't find me, either.

"Toto, you dumb dog!" I called. "How come you only rescue me when I don't need rescuing?" I sprinted down to the end of the path and made another turn. I kept running, hearing Casimir's footsteps behind me, until I ended up facing a wall of unbroken hedges.

I whirled around and dashed back onto the path.

Casimir was just running out of another dead end. His back was to me and he started to run in the opposite direction. I didn't move until he disappeared around a corner.

Then I started to run again.

"I will catch you, my little honey hive!" Casimir cried.

"Not if I can help it, hummingbird-stuffer!"

"The thrill of the chase!" he shouted. "It arouses my capillaries! What do I get if I find you?"

*"Dead capillaries!"*

I raced through an opening in the solid green wall and skidded to a stop. I groaned. I was surrounded on three sides by hedges. There was a goldfish pond in the center of this section, with a white bench in front of the pond.

I was gasping for breath. But I couldn't stop. Casimir's voice was too close.

I headed back the way I had come in. Just as I hit the break in the hedge, Casimir popped up in front of me.

"Toto!" he cried triumphantly. He tagged me on the shoulder. "You are 'it' now."

142

He grabbed me around the waist in a bear hug. "What a fun game! I will kiss you passionately about the face and then we will play again."

"Over my dead body," I panted. Casimir was hardly even winded. "You make me barf, Prince."

"Woof, woof," he said playfully, and kissed me on the nose.

Casimir lifted me up by the elbows as easily as if I were Dolores's stuffed Snoopy.

"Put me down!"

He tried to kiss me on the lips. I twisted my head away.

"TOTO!" I screamed.

"Yes, we will play Toto again," Casimir said. He started walking toward the bench beside the goldfish pond, still dangling me off the ground by my elbows.

"But first, I will pelt you with hot kisses."

*"I'd rather make out with a mongoose."* I drew my foot back and kicked him in the knee with the toe of my boot.

"Ouch!" But he didn't drop me.

So I kneecapped him with my other boot.

Before he could say ouch, Toto, my semi-faithful dog, bounded through the hedge.

"Toto! You certainly took your own sweet time."

"Perhaps we will play a different game," the prince said. "You did not tell me all the rules."

Toto took a flying leap at Casimir. His front paws landed on the prince's shoulders, and all three of us went sprawling into the fish pond.

"Good dog!" I cheered. "You can watch all the Lassie movies you want."

Casimir spluttered and spouted water as he began

to rant in some language I didn't understand. Maybe Arcanian. Definitely unprintable.

I was soaked from the waist down and Casimir was soggy all over. His face was red with rage.

"I trust your little dip cooled you off?" I asked, struggling to my feet. I stepped out of the pond and patted Toto's head. "I'm going to get you a medal of valor," I promised him. "We'll have a whole award ceremony and everything."

Casimir crawled out of the water. He grabbed his knee, where I had kicked him, and winced.

"The dog," he said threateningly, "will not accompany us on our honeymoon."

"Don't worry. Neither will I."

# 18

"You will not have to see Casimir anymore," the princess said.

"Thank you," I said fervently. "I'll go right back into princess training, and from now on —"

"Until the wedding," she finished.

"ARRGGH! I don't believe it! How could that evil toad still want to marry me?"

"It beats us," said the prince.

That was the day of the maze disaster, and Casimir's fiery protests to my royal parents.

For the last two weeks, I'd been locked up tighter than Fort Knox.

Two guards stood at attention outside my room

night and day. They followed me everywhere I went in the palace. When I went outside to play with Toto, they followed me. Even walking from my room to the sewing room, where Mlle Chenille was making frighteningly good progress on my bridal gown, they followed me, guarding the outside door until the fitting was over.

The princess gave the palace switchboard operator orders that I was not allowed to receive any phone calls.

She confiscated my mousse.

"And I wouldn't get my heart set on that medal of valor," I told Toto.

At least they hadn't confiscated Toto.

Mme Banat resumed my lessons. She was supposed to be drilling me on the intricacies of the wedding ceremony and explaining my duties at the Gloxinia Festival. But I spent most of the time pouring out my feelings to her, pleading for help, and crying.

She was sympathetic. But all she did was shake her head and look troubled.

"I can't help you, Your Highness. Believe me, I'd like to, but there's nothing I can do."

"You could call my parents. You could phone from your house."

She shook her head helplessly. "All the operators have been forbidden to place calls to the United States. I'm very upset by your situation. I don't like what I see happening."

"I'm *scared*."

She put her arm around me. "Do you know what my name means?" she asked gently.

"No." What did that have to do with anything?

"*Banat* is a symbol of freedom for Rumanians. I'm very proud of my name."

"I would be, too," I agreed. "Look, maybe you could see Geoffrey. He might be able to help me escape."

"I've seen Geoffrey." She kept her voice low. "He's terribly upset. He can't get within a hundred feet of the palace without being turned back. He tried to leave the country in hopes of contacting your parents, but he was stopped at the border."

"It's hopeless," I moaned.

Mme Banat nodded. "They've even blocked all the roads to the valley until the festival. You couldn't get out of Dulsia even if you were able to get out of the palace."

"I'm *doomed*."

Mlle Chenille was interviewed on *Saxony Coburn Tonight* about the wedding gown she designed for me. She looked very nervous. I didn't understand anything she said after, *"C'est magnifique."*

I already knew what the gown looked like. It had alternating tiers of satin and lace, gathered with fake gloxinia buds. No hoops.

And it was almost done. Mlle Chenille's assistants just had to finish hemming the twelve-foot train.

My wedding was three days away. I'd been trying to plot an escape for two weeks, but it was like running through the maze. I just kept hitting dead ends, no matter which way my mind turned.

Poor Dolores, I thought, as I watched Mlle Chenille. Even if she is a spying little stool pigeon. That gown was designed for her. She must feel as miserable as I do over this wedding.

No, almost as miserable. No one could out-miserable me right now.

The camera cut away from Mlle Chenille to a shot of a large platform completely draped with flowers. I could see wheels underneath. A worker was fixing a stool right in the center.

The royal float.

A second stool was placed on the float, and immediately two women started covering the stools with more flowers.

I'll have to sit there with Casimir for the parade.

Dolores! I thought again. Why didn't I think of her before?

She and I had exactly the same problem. She wanted to marry Casimir and I didn't want to marry Casimir. I would do anything to stop this wedding — if I could think of anything to do — and she'd do anything to stop it if *she* could think of anything to do.

Dolores could go to Geoffrey. No one would stop her.

But Mme Banat had already tried Geoffrey. What good would it do to send him a note that said *HELP!!!?* There was no way he could help.

All the roads would be sealed off until the festival, so —

Wait a minute. *Until* the festival. The roads would have to be open the day of the wedding. How else would the tourists get into the city for Saxony Coburn's most festive Gloxinia Festival ever?

All Geoffrey had to do was hide his moped — or a jeep, if he could get one — near a road down to the valley. . . .

We'd be cutting it awfully close. Talk about last-minute escapes; this was ridiculous. Even if we did manage to get down the mountain without being caught by the army, how would we get past the border guards?

This plan has a million holes in it, I thought glumly.

But it was the only plan I had.

Dolores was watching *Saxony Coburn Tonight* as Toto and I walked into her room. She was sitting on a chaise longue, with Snoopy clutched to her bosom.

"I'm getting married in the morning," I sang cheerily. "Hi, Dolores."

"She does not knock, Snoopy. And she brings in her savage killer dog."

"I want to talk to you," I said.

"You are right, Snoopy. We will not talk to the arrogant American invader. We will watch television and count the hours until our lifelong dream curdles like rancid goat milk."

I shrugged. "Okay, Toto. Don't say I didn't try."

She can talk to *her* dog, I can talk to *my* dog.

"I wanted to tell her about how that letter from the doctor was a forgery, and that she's the real princess after all, but if she's just going to speak to her stuffed animal. . . . "

Dolores leaped out of the chaise longue and

flipped Snoopy out the open window.

"Let's talk, American buddy. Sisterhood is powerful. Right on."

"Everyone is so surprised," Mme Banat told me the next day. "Dolores suddenly decided to come out of seclusion. I'm taking her shopping this afternoon. The prince and princess are so happy that she's recovered."

"Gosh!" I said. "Isn't that a startling turn of events?"

Mme Banat eyed me suspiciously. "I have the feeling that there is something about this I don't know. I like the feeling. Don't spoil it."

Okay. I won't tell her about the detailed note Dolores will carry to the newspaper office. Or the note and map she'll bring back to me — if Geoffrey really loves me.

I'll just sit here quietly and try to figure out how I'm going to ride down a mountain pass on the back of a moped, in a wedding gown with a twelve-foot train.

## 19

"Happy birthday to me, happy birthday to me." It sounded like a funeral march the way I sang it.

"Here comes the bride, all dressed in white," the prince sang gaily. "Prince Casimir will be beside himself when he sees you."

As long as *I'm* not beside him, I don't care where he is.

Mlle Chenille, Jeannot, and two assistants fluttered around me, making last-minute adjustments in my gown.

"*Magnifique*, Mlle Chenille! *Un triomphe!*" Princess Florinda swept into my chamber, flanked by two guards. She was holding a deep blue velvet cushion in both hands, like a tray.

"One look at his beautiful bride and the prince will forget about those silly rumors," she told Prince Albert.

"Silly rumors?" I brightened up for the first time since daybreak. "What silly rumors?" I'd only made up the forgery story to give Dolores a motive for helping me, but maybe she'd spread it around.

"Do not worry, dear," the princess said. "Everything will go perfectly."

*Not if I can help it.*

"Now look what we have for you."

She held out the cushion. Arranged on the blue velvet was a massive silver necklace dripping with sapphires. It was more like a collar than a necklace. The gems were set in three rows that radiated out from the heavy silver like spokes in a wheel.

"This is for me?" I gasped.

"Part of the crown jewels. You will wear them today, but someday they will be yours."

The princess fastened the collar around my neck. It thunked against my collarbone like a cold, iron noose.

I looked at myself in the mirror. "Fan*tas*tic."

One of the guards handed the princess a large velvet box. She opened it and took out a small diamond tiara. She placed the tiara on my head.

"Ahh," breathed Jeannot. Mlle Chenille hurried to my side with the yards of tulle that made up my bridal veil. She started attaching the veil to the tiara and the tiara to my hair.

It seemed to take forever. When she was finally satisfied, she stood back, her hands clasped together, her face shining with pride.

*"Mon chef d'oeuvre!"* she exclaimed.

I certainly was a masterpiece. I was beautiful. For the first time since I'd been in Saxony Coburn, I looked like a princess.

I was so caught up in the dazzling image that looked back at me from the mirror, that for a moment I forgot about Casimir, forgot that I'd been held incommunicado for two weeks, forgot that I was only hours away from a harebrained attempt to flee Saxony Coburn.

I just smiled dreamily at my reflection, the way I used to dream over the illustrations of princesses in my fairy tale books.

"And I haven't even got any makeup on," I marveled.

"Jeannot will help you with that now," the princess said. "Jeannot, *le maquillage. Un peu, c'est tout.* Just a little, my dear," she told me. "You only need some color in your cheeks. You look quite pale."

I came back to reality with a thud. This is no fairy tale, I reminded myself. No time now to dream about fairy princesses.

Everyone cleared out of my chamber, leaving Jeannot and me by ourselves. Poor Toto had been put in an outdoor kennel for the day. The princess didn't want him anywhere near me while I had on a bridal gown and a twelve-foot train.

I had bidden him a tearful farewell early in the morning. Nobody but me realized why it was so tearful. I might never see him again.

Mme Banat had come to wish me happy birthday

and good luck right after breakfast. I hugged her hard. "Whatever happens, I'll miss you," I told her. "You're a true friend."

Jeannot brushed a little blusher on my cheeks and rubbed some pale lip gloss over my mouth. She ranted excitedly in French, oohing and aahing as she worked.

"I want to be alone for a few minutes, Jeannot," I told her when she finished. *"Je voudrais être seule."*

"Yes, yes," she nodded. "I dig it. I will rest outside the door."

Her English had improved. I'd miss Jeannot, too.

As soon as she shut the door behind herself, I kicked off the white satin slippers I was wearing and stuffed them behind the bed pillows.

I reached into the closet and pulled out my sneakers.

The entire palace staff was lined up in the reception foyer as Casimir and I posed for wedding pictures on the stairway.

Just like the first day I came to Saxony Coburn, I thought. How differently things would have turned out if only Casimir had not been a prerequisite to princesshood. I would have been a very benevolent ruler. Firm, but fair.

I would have figured out a way to pump up the economy. I'd have gotten this principality modernized and industrialized and had a cable TV franchise within two years. Three, tops.

"Isn't this bad luck?" I asked, as Casimir put his hand on my shoulder. "The groom isn't supposed to see the bride before the ceremony."

"Pish tush," Prince Albert said. "We are not old fogies here. Do not be superstitious."

I shrugged. "Okay." After all, it would be worse luck if my groom got to see his bride *after* the ceremony.

"Have I told you," Casimir said, as Mlle Chenille bent down to arrange the train, "that you look excessively splenderous?"

"About six times," I said nervously.

I could hear the revelers outside the palace. The Gloxinia Festival was underway.

The prince bent down to whisper in my ear, and the palace staff giggled and sighed and began to get silly. *"Un baiser!"* someone urged. *"Un baiser!"*

"The menial servants wish me to kiss you," Casimir said, "but I do not think it would be dignified."

"Me, neither," I agreed.

"Nothing would convince me," he murmured, "that you are not of royal blood."

So there *were* rumors, and Casimir had heard them!

If only I'd thought of enlisting Dolores's help sooner, we could have had time to stir up some real uncertainty about which one of us was the true princess.

I might have been able to reach my parents, Casimir might have postponed the wedding, and I wouldn't have had to resort to this drastic, eleventh-hour flight to freedom.

"And now," Prince Albert said, after the photographer finished, "a special surprise." He opened a flat leather case about the size of a notebook.

"Your stamp was officially issued today." He held up a block of stamps with my face on them. "Here are the first sheets, hot off the press."

I was speechless.

That was me, all right, in profile, my neck and head, engraved in gloxinia purple. SAXONY was printed in black above my head, and COBURN below it. Right under my neck it said, 10 z. (for zelwigs).

It's a weird feeling to see yourself on a postage stamp, just like a queen or a president or a famous disease.

"Awesome," I whispered. "Totally awesome."

M. Blitzen handed me a pouch. "They will sell nicely," he said. "But we think the royal wedding stamps will do even better."

"What's this?" I asked, taking the pouch.

"For the servants," the princess said. "You will give them each a stamp as a souvenir of this day."

"One stamp?"

She nodded. "They will treasure it forever."

For the second time in four weeks I worked my way down the line of the palace staff. This time, Casimir was at my side and Mlle Chenille's assistants followed behind me, trying to keep my train rolled up.

I handed each person a stamp and they bowed and curtseyed and murmured excitedly. Personally I felt a little silly about the whole thing. I was sure there were things they would treasure a lot more than a ten-zelwig stamp. Like a week off, for instance, or an extra paycheck.

156

The princess led us out to a balcony overlooking the palace square, where I had first arrived in Saxony Coburn. A throng of people in plastic raincoats filled the square, and as the prince and princess opened the glass doors, a great cheer went up.

The four of us waved and smiled at the happy crowd. I felt like an awful hypocrite, greeting my subjects with a cheerful wave only two hours before I was going to desert them and destroy their economy.

"I think it is about time," said the princess. "Don't you, Albert?"

My heart started to race wildly. I grabbed the edge of the balcony to keep from fainting.

"Time for what?" I choked.

"Time for us to take our places on the reviewing stand," the prince said. "We will watch the festivities from there."

Casimir took my arm. His sword glanced off the skirt of my gown. He stepped around me and took my other arm.

"Come, my celestial whiteness. The parade cannot commence itself without us."

*Geoffrey*, I pleaded silently. I know you're risking everything for me if you go through with this. *But don't fail me now.*

The reviewing stand was set up opposite the palace, across the road from the square. The floats came toward us from town, turned in front of the reviewing stand, and proceeded through the palace gates and off to one side of the great lawn.

People lined both sides of the street and filled the square. I scanned the crowds for Geoffrey. If he was there, I couldn't pick him out.

And where's Dolores? I wondered. The only people with us in the reviewing stand were Prince Albert and Princess Florinda, M. Creanga, and M. Blitzen.

Mme Banat was watching from a palace window, along with most of the staff.

I tried to look interested as a float titled *"SAXONY COBURN AUJOURD'HUI"* (Saxony Coburn Today) turned in front of the stand. My father was right, I thought. It didn't seem to be much different from the float called *"SAXONY COBURN HIER"* (Yesterday).

After the floats were all lined up on the lawns, we were supposed to speed to the far side of town in a Mercedes, mount the royal float, and be paraded back through town to the square, where the ceremony would be performed on the float.

I figured they must have put in some more stools since I'd seen the float on TV.

And sometime between now and then, Geoffrey was supposed to create a diversion.

The float saluting three hundred years of sausage-casing making came toward us. I was so nervous I couldn't stop tapping the wooden floor of the stand with the toes of my sneakers. But I was a little curious about how they could depict sausage-casing making with gloxinias, delphiniums, and ferns.

Not very well, I concluded, as the float passed

us. Five workers dressed in white imitated mechanical men on an assembly line, handing chains of flowers along to the next worker with jerky, robotlike movements.

It was getting awfully hot. My gown was so heavy, the sapphire necklace chafed me — the jewels! I remembered. The princess will think I stole them!

I'll mail them back as soon as I get home, I decided.

Insured.

Geoffrey sure was leaving things to the last minute. There were only two floats left to go before I was on display. I just hate split-second timing.

I don't know how many movies I've seen where someone sets a bomb to go off in three minutes, and then has to get out of the building, or the mine, or whatever he's blowing up, in two minutes and fifty-nine seconds.

You *know* something's going to go wrong. A broken leg, a cave-in, a block in the escape route — some sort of unexpected hitch is going to trap this guy. And I sit there watching his face get all sweaty, and the fuse growing shorter and shorter, and I think, *Dummy!* You couldn't have set the bomb to go off in half an hour?

That's how I felt now as the last float, dedicated to Princess Florinda and Prince Albert, sped by. It didn't really speed by. The floats were only going about two miles an hour, but that's the way it seemed to me.

Maybe Geoffrey isn't going to help me escape, I thought. Even though his note back to me had said,

"A-OK. I love you." Maybe he'd changed his mind. Maybe he'd gotten scared. Maybe he didn't love me enough.

Maybe the royal family had thrown him in the dungeon until after the wedding.

No, no, it was too horrible to think about. Geoffrey would rescue me. He was just waiting for the right moment. He probably reasoned that it would be too hard for me to escape from the reviewing stand, so he was waiting until —

Waiting until *what?*

No matter how he created a diversion, there'd be an awful lot of people surrounding me until after the wedding service. How was I going to elude them all and run off to the spot Geoffrey had marked on the map?

Casimir wouldn't just stand there and do nothing as I ran off — or waddled off, considering the pounds of satin, lace, and gems I was wearing.

Casimir would probably yell, "Toto!" and run right after me.

"Come, my lovebirds," the princess said. "It is time."

# 20

I am not here, I told myself.

This Tony Perkins look-alike standing beside me is not going to be my husband. That man in front of us, speaking French and Latin, is not a priest. This canopy dripping with gloxinias, hibiscus, and wisteria does not drip for me; it drips for somebody else.

*Geoffrey, where's the diversion already?* This is getting ridiculous. We're down to the wire. In five minutes I'm going to be Mrs. Casimir the Creep, unless I try and respond *non* when I'm supposed to say *oui.*

I do *not* take this prince to be my lawfully wed-ded husband. In fact, this wedding is probably *un*lawful in sixty free-world countries.

*"C'est une trompe,"* I said, when the priest paused for a moment. *"C'est une erreur. Il est une* Big Mistake."

The priest looked up, startled. Casimir gripped my arm. *"Sois tranquille,"* he said. "Be entirely calm. All is well."

"All is *not* well," I said desperately. "All stinks on ice. I'm not going through with this."

Prince Albert patted my hand. "It is a jim dandy wedding so far. Do not louse it up. *Continuez,"* he told the priest.

The priest hesitated. He asked something in French. Princess Florinda answered in French. The priest looked doubtful, but he *continuez*ed.

I began to recognize some of the things the priest was saying. Mme Banat had drilled me, so that I would be familiar with each part of the ceremony and be ready with the right responses.

We're getting down to the crunch. Even if I give the wrong responses, it won't do me any good. This priest doesn't speak English. The princess will tell him I don't speak French. No matter what I say, *I'm going to end up married to a taxidermist.*

You failed me, Geoffrey, I thought sadly. All right, I didn't expect the white horse and the shining armor — that's only in fairy tales — but was it too much to ask for a moped?

*"L'alliance,"* the priest announced.

The ring.

Casimir reached into his pocket.

"HELP!" I screamed. *"Aidez-moi!* I'm not your princess. *Je suis une* fake."

The princess shrieked. Casimir began shouting in Arcanian. The crowd surged toward us, making extremely ugly noises and hurling gloxinias at us.

Good thing for me that tomatoes were not Saxony Coburn's national plant.

Just then, someone screamed, *"Le palais! En feu! En feu!"*

Everyone began pointing and shouting.

Sure enough, black smoke was billowing out of a second-floor window of the palace.

The servants who had been watching from the palace disappeared. Suddenly, from the smoke-filled window, a huge banner unfurled. In black paint, it read: ABBY ADAMS, *IMPOSTEUR*!! YANKEE GO HOME!

Dolores is no slouch with a bedsheet herself, I thought.

Hey! Why am I standing here like an iceberg? *This is the diversion.*

A volley of shots rang out somewhere in the crowd.

*"Assassins!"* the cry went up. *"Assassins!"*

"Duck!" Prince Albert ordered. "Take cover."

The crowd started to scatter in all directions, screaming in panic. The prince, the princess, Casimir, and the priest threw themselves down to the flower-strewn floor of the float.

A second volley of shots erupted.

"We are being assaulted!" the princess cried. "Dolores, get down! Save yourself!"

"You bet I will!" I jumped off the float.

I raced toward the reviewing stand, trying to hold up the skirt of my gown. Everyone was running away from the square in opposite directions. My train dragged behind me, and I tried to gather it up as I ran.

I was sure that the "assassins" were only strings of firecrackers. I knew no one was trying to shoot me. I trotted past the reviewing stand toward the road Geoffrey had marked on his map.

"Abby!" He sprang out from behind a bush.

"Geoffrey! My *hero*!"

"I love you," he said. "Let's move out."

"I love you, too," I said. "Nifty diversion."

"I saw it in an American movie. I commandeered a jeep. It's behind that bush. Here we go."

We leaped into the jeep. He leaped, I climbed. My bridal gown spread across the entire front seat. I bunched my train on my lap.

"You take up too much room," he complained. He tried to push the layers of satin and lace out of the way.

"They wouldn't let me wear jeans for the wedding."

The jeep's engine roared to life and Geoffrey pulled out onto the unpaved road.

"It's going to be bumpy going down the mountain," he warned.

"It's already bumpy."

"And very steep. But I've driven it before."

"I have complete confidence in you. I came up here in a helicopter. If I lived through that, a little mountain isn't going to throw me. Do you think we'll be able to get across the border?"

"I don't know, but we'll give it our best shot."

Boy, did he sound different. He looked different, too. He had on a khaki bush jacket and a red neckerchief. His eyes were fixed on the road as he concentrated on steering, but he had a big, excited grin on his face as we barreled down the road.

"This is just like *Raiders!*" he shouted.

Good grief! He's playing Indiana Jones.

"Oh, no!" he cried.

A land rover with a bunch of people in it was heading straight at us.

"Get out of the way!" he shouted. "Move over! *Allez, allez!*"

The road wasn't wide enough for the cars to pass each other.

"Geoffrey, pull over!"

"They might be soldiers. I can't see *who* they are."

"Slow down, at least! Getting killed isn't part of my plan."

He slowed down and the land rover slowed down, too.

"This may be it, Your Highness," he said. "I just want you to know, they'll never take you alive."

"Gee, thanks."

"I mean, not while *I'm* alive."

"They're not wearing uniforms." I squinted at the people in the land rover. "I think they're just tourists."

I could see a man, two women, and a boy in the vehicle. They certainly didn't look very dangerous. In fact, three of them looked like —

"It's my folks!" I whooped. "Geoffrey, that's my *family*!"

I vaulted over the side of the jeep and started running.

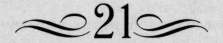

# 21

"What was the name of Donald O'Connor's co-star in six films?"

Teddy looked at me blankly. "Who's Donald O'Connor?"

"I know, I know!" said Geoffrey. "Francis the Talking Mule." He'd already won nine games of Trivial Pursuit, and was working on his last wedge in this one.

Geoffrey, Teddy, Dolores, and I had been sitting in a room down the hall from the War Room for a day and a half now. Inside the War Room the princess, the prince, M. Creanga, M. Blitzen, Prince Casimir, my parents, and Congresswoman Marianne

Wayne were engaged in marathon negotiations.

Every once in a while, Geoffrey's father was called in. He seemed like a nice man, but he constantly looked worried. Each time he came out of the War Room, he looked more worried.

Geoffrey asked him, "What's happening now, Papa?" and he would just shake his head and mutter.

Whenever any of them came out of the War Room we asked, "What's happening?" But no one talked to us in specifics. My mother would say, "This is total craziness, but don't worry. Everything's going to be fine."

My father would say, "Chin up. Ms. Wayne's doing a great job."

And Congresswoman Wayne would say, "Hold the good thought, honey. Wayne's on your side. This isn't going to hurt our next campaign a bit."

Dolores was going crazy. I couldn't blame her. I figured that with my parents and our congresswoman here, I was safe. It was Dolores's whole life that hung in the balance.

Finally Geoffrey was summoned.

"Why do they need me?" he said nervously.

"Why don't they need *me*?" I said. "I'm the princess, for heaven's sake. You'd think they'd want a little of my input."

Dolores looked pained. Geoffrey went off to the War Room.

"Good," Teddy said. "Now maybe someone else can get a wedge."

Dolores stood up and threw her blue game wheel across the room. "I cannot concentrate on this silly game until I know if I will marry a prince or a pauper."

It took about a hundred years until Geoffrey came back. He looked dazed, but wildly happy.

"What is it?" Dolores demanded. "Is it decided?"

"I'm a hero," he said weakly. "I'm a national hero. I saved the country from the false princess. No offense, Abby," he added, nodding in my direction.

"I'm *it*?" Dolores screamed. *"I'm the princess?"*

Geoffrey nodded again. He looked as if he'd just returned from Oz.

"YIPPEE!" Dolores shot out of the room like a rocket. "Casimir! Where are you, Sugar Lips? Come and kiss your bride! Is the priest still here?"

My parents and Congresswoman Wayne limped in, smiling broadly. They raised their clasped hands in a victory salute.

"It's incredible," my mother said. "Ms. Wayne was an absolute *dynamo*."

"But what happened?" I asked. "How come I'm not princess anymore?"

"It's the most amazing thing," my father said. "It seems you were never switched at birth at all."

*"What?* How did they find that out?"

"The doctor's letter was forged," Ms. Wayne said.

"But that's not true —" Oops. I was about to say that I started that rumor myself. Or Dolores did, after I made it up. I glanced guiltily at Geoffrey. Geoffrey looked up at the ceiling.

"Mr. Torunga sent the letter to a newspaper in Switzerland," Ms. Wayne said. "I had a handwriting expert standing by in Switzerland to analyze it. He matched it to samples of the doctor's handwriting, and said the letter was a definite forgery."

*"Really?"* I said.

*"Really?"* Geoffrey repeated. He looked more dazed than ever.

"The forger even confessed," my mother said. "She was the nurse who worked for Dr. Zdenka."

"But why?" I asked.

"It was a political thing," the congresswoman replied. "She's — what did they call her? Anti-Gloxinian?"

"Ahh," Geoffrey nodded. "That could explain it. Though it's out of character for an Anti-Gloxinian to wait sixteen years for a plot to hatch. They're only a small fringe group but they're very hot-tempered."

"This is incredible," I muttered. "I mean, you guys don't know *how* incredible. I made up that story my —"

Geoffrey cleared his throat.

"Your Former Highness," he said. "You asked me to help rescue you from Prince Casimir. I'm a national hero for preventing your wedding. Would you please put a lid on it now?"

I nodded. "Good thinking."

"Abby's not a princess anymore?" Teddy said. "Good deal. I'm glad."

*"You're* glad?" My mother laughed. "Princess Florinda and Prince Albert are overjoyed."

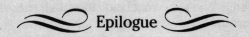 Epilogue

And that's the way it really happened, no matter what you read in the papers.

I'm still not convinced that I'm not a princess. It seems to me that the last-minute discovery of the "forged" letter was pretty convenient all around.

But I'll never be sure.

I did get to take Toto home with me. Dolores was afraid of him and Casimir didn't want him — at least, not alive — so he's home with me, where he belongs.

And I have my stamps as souvenirs of my brief reign.

Geoffrey writes to me every week, and he's

planning on coming to visit in the fall. I miss him so much. I dream about him almost all the time, but I've been pretty busy with magazine interviews and the mini-series.

We signed a contract with Ersatz Productions because they offered enough money to put me through veterinary school.

I'm a little nervous about the show, though. Ersatz is making a few "minor changes" which they claim will "enhance the exploitation value."

They've made me twenty-six instead of fifteen and eleven twelfths. They're trying to sign Morgan Fairchild for the dual role of me and Dolores.

They're emphasizing the Anti-Gloxinian terrorists, but they're calling them Communists.

They want to make Geoffrey's firecracker diversion a real assassination. They decided my fake suicide wasn't dramatic enough, so they have me really try to kill myself, which is totally out of character for me.

They're getting Benji to play the part of Toto.

I'm kind of upset that they're changing what really happened to me into something so totally unreal.

I mean, who's going to believe a story like that?

Ellen Conford has been delighting teenage audiences for years with such funny, upbeat stories as *If This Is Love, I'll Take Spaghetti*; *Dear Lovey Hart, I Am Desperate*; *Seven Days to a Brand-New Me*; and *We Interrupt This Semester For an Important Bulletin* (all available from Scholastic). Whether writing about first love, or a girl who becomes an "instant princess," Ellen Conford is always on target with sensitivity and humor about the crises that arise in young people's lives. While she has never been a princess, Ellen Conford has worn the crown of Scrabble champion. She lives in Great Neck, New York.